Because of the Rain

of the

by DEBORAH RANEY

For Vicky, Brad, and Beverly
who shared a perfect childhood with me;
and in memory of our sister Kim,
who tasted heaven before us all.

"To appoint unto them that mourn...to give unto them beauty for ashes, the oil of joy for mourning, the garment of praise for the spirit of heaviness; that they might be called trees of righteousness, the planting of the Lord, that he might be glorified" (Isaiah 61:3)

One

Anna Marquette stepped into the quiet of the carpeted hallway and closed the door to the hotel room behind her. Checking the lock, she tucked the key card into her large leather handbag and headed across the hall toward the bank of elevators. The doors at the far end of the row slid open silently, and she entered the empty car. The air inside smelled of stale cigarette smoke and air conditioning. Anna pressed the button for the lobby and leaned back against the handrail as the elevator began its descent. The elevator shaft was encased in glass, affording Anna a sweeping view of Orlando's skyline as the cage crept slowly down the sleek face of the towering building and ground to a halt on the lobby level.

It was March, and they'd flown out of Chicago's O'Hare yesterday morning in below freezing temperatures. But March in Orlando meant ninety degrees. The late afternoon sun beat down on the glass, warming Anna's bare arms. It always amazed her that the weather could be so drastically different just a few hours' flight away.

Paul had laughed at Anna as she packed sweaters and wool jackets alongside her summer dresses.

"Anna, we're going to Florida, not the Yukon."

"I know, but I'm not taking any chances. You know I can't stand to be cold."

"Suit yourself. But I'm only carrying one suitcase." He gave her the grin that had won her heart twenty-three years ago and continued folding golf shirts and summer dress shirts, adeptly packing them into one half of the large suitcase that lay open on their bed.

An executive with a large advertising agency in Chicago, Paul Marquette was a seasoned traveler. His business trips were usually overnight—two or three days at the most—but he traveled several times a month. Whenever he had to be gone longer than that, he liked Anna to come with him.

When their daughters were younger, Anna had relished the chance to get away with Paul and take a break from being a full-time mom. Her parents lived an hour west of Chicago and were always eager for a chance to spoil their granddaughters. But now that the girls were grown and on their own, and Anna's days were more her own to orchestrate, the days spent lounging in a hotel room or shopping the malls of whatever city they happened to be in had lost some of their appeal. Yet the evenings with Paul, exploring the city together and sampling the local cuisine, made the days of solitude worthwhile.

And now that she'd gone back to school, Anna knew that for a few years at least, she would no longer be able to drop everything and take off with her husband whenever she pleased. Fortunately, this trip had fallen during the university's spring break.

Anna was teaching first grade when she and Paul met, and she'd kept her teaching job after their marriage, but when Kara was born two years later, Anna was smitten. Although she'd always planned to go back to her job when her maternity leave was over, as the scheduled day of her return to the classroom crept closer, she could not imagine leaving this precious little bundle with *anyone*, let alone a series of relative strangers at the local daycare.

Paul was surprised at her change of heart, but they'd reworked their budget and decided Anna would stay home with the baby a while longer.

She was still at home when Kassandra came along two years later. And then two years had stretched into almost twenty, until the girls were grown.

Anna had thoroughly enjoyed the busy and fulfilling life of a stay-at-home mom. But when Kara started her senior year of high school, Anna realized how quickly the empty nest was approaching, and she started to think about what she wanted to do with her life once the girls were grown and gone. Teaching had lost its appeal, and while she'd briefly entertained thoughts of going to medical school, the realization that she would be past fifty by the time she could begin a practice sobered her. Now, at forty-five, she was back in college studying for a master's degree in counseling. A whole new, intriguing world had opened up to her at the university, and Anna was enthusiastically working toward the day when she could open her own clinical practice.

She was grateful for Paul's support through it all. He'd shared her enthusiasm from the beginning, along with her passion for the study of psychology. "Advertising is nothing more than the exploration and application of the remarkable ways the human mind works," he'd told her more than once. Her studies had precipitated many animated—if sometimes heated—discussions between them.

The elevator doors glided open, and Anna stepped into the cool marble-floored lobby. She pushed open the heavy front door to a blast of Florida heat. The bellman indicated that the taxi she'd summoned was already parked under the canopy in front of the hotel. She thanked him and climbed into the waiting cab. "Longwood Center, please."

The driver grunted his acknowledgment and eased into the flow of traffic on the congested boulevard. Anna had arranged to meet Paul for dinner at eight o'clock. Friends had recommended an Italian restaurant near the shopping center, but Anna had left early enough to do a little shopping beforehand. The warm weather had put her in the mood to buy summer clothes. Paul would never let her hear the end of it if she walked into the restaurant with a shopping bag full of summer things. Oh well, his teasing was one of the things that had drawn her to Paul. And thanks to her father, who was a terrible tease, Anna had always seen teasing as a sign of affection.

The cab pulled smoothly alongside the curb of the shopping center. Anna paid the fare and tipped the driver, then entered the huge mall, which was nearly empty on a weekday afternoon. The shops were situated around an open courtyard that boasted an abundance of fragrant flowering trees and a cobblestone floor. The subdued staccato of Anna's sandals on the cobblestone mingled with the musical splashing of the courtyard's many fountains and the hushed conversations of scattered shoppers.

Enjoying the balmy weather and window-shopping, Anna walked at a leisurely pace to the far end of the mall. When she turned to retrace her steps, she got down to business, entering several shops that looked promising and even trying on a few items. She bought three shirts and an expensive pair of sunglasses. Then, feeling guilty that she'd spent too much money, she carried her bags to the food court in the center of the courtyard.

She ordered iced tea and, juggling the brimming cup and her packages, made her way to a small table. She sat there entranced by the parade of people passing by. She'd always been enthralled with the diversity and uniqueness of people, but her study of psychology had made the observing even more fascinating. It was such fun to hazard guesses about personalities and relationships—and often be proved wrong in only a few minutes of observation. If she'd learned one thing, it was that you could not judge a book by its cover.

She checked her watch. It was almost time to meet Paul.

Taking one last sip from the tall Styrofoam cup, she gathered up her packages. Pushing back the chair, she surveyed her surroundings, unsure which entrance would take her in the direction of the restaurant. She'd spotted *Italia* from the taxi as they pulled onto the mall's frontage road, but she had her directions turned around in this city.

She headed toward the entrance where the cab had dropped her. Traffic in the parking lot was picking up now that the workday had ended. The sun had sunk below the horizon an hour earlier, and Anna looked around, trying to orient herself.

The restaurant was nowhere in sight. It must be on the opposite side of the mall. Sighing, she turned to go back through the shopping center's doors, then decided it would be just as quick to walk around the outside of the complex. Besides, the weather was glorious. She followed the narrow walk and came to the end of the long row of buildings.

Rounding the corner, she spotted the restaurant. *Italia* declared a large banner flapping in the breeze at the center of a spotlighted avenue of red, white, and green flags. The restaurant was much farther from Longwood Center than it had looked from the window of the taxi. She'd have to cross a busy street and walk past another small office complex to get there.

The lights of the city twinkled in the semidarkness, and the streetlights illuminating the outside of the mall grew fewer and farther between as she walked away from the anchor stores' facades.

She approached a service entrance. A huge air conditioning unit jutted out into the path, and several trash bins were clustered in the darkened alley that led, she supposed, into the shopping center's maintenance area. In the warmth of the evening, the trash bins emitted a pungent odor. Wrinkling her nose and checking the drive for traffic, Anna stepped off the curb.

Because of the Rain

Two

She hoped Paul hadn't been waiting long. Waiting had never been his strong suit. Intent on the maze of sidewalks and crossings leading to the other side of the busy boulevard, Anna walked past the service entrance at Longwood Center, trying not to inhale the foul odors coming from the dumpsters.

She inhaled sharply as a figure suddenly loomed in front of her. Without warning, a sharp pain tore through her left shoulder, and before she had time to even imagine what had struck her, she felt a heavy cloth close over her head. Arms flailing, she went down, then felt herself being dragged across the concrete. At first she thought she'd been hit by a car. But hearing a man's voice—no, more like gutteral grunts—she fought against the panic rising in her throat.

A heady rush of adrenaline surged through her veins and she tried to get loose, regain her footing. But a muscular arm hooked her neck, and she felt herself being lifted until her toes barely touched the ground. She tried to scream, but the vice around her throat nearly crushed her windpipe, rendering her mute. A sickly sweet smell assaulted her nostrils. Men's cologne mingled with sweat, she thought. She struggled to push down the panic and think clearly, but her thoughts ran wild. Waves of pain rolled over her, so intense she feared she'd lose consciousness.

"Hush, Mam'selle." For the first time, her attacker spoke. "You cooperate, no? Then maybe you walk out of here een one piece." He had a deep voice and the smile his voice held belied the threat of his words. He spoke deliberately, in a heavy tongue that sounded French to Anna's ear.

Her thoughts churned, disconnected, in her mind. She struggled to loose her arm from the man's grip, but that only made him squeeze more tightly, wrenching her arm backward. And then she felt the smooth, hard, cold of steel against her neck. Her thought of the blade on her throat erased the pain that seared through her shoulder.

She willed herself to stay calm. "Please," she pled in a hoarse whisper. "There's...there's some money in my purse." She tried to thrust her handbag in the direction of the voice, but she couldn't make her arms work right. "Just take it. Take all of it."

"Ah, miss, your money eez not what I am after." His voice came from above her and held a wicked sneer. He must be tall. She fought to memorize every detail. She could see nothing but felt the smooth, flimsy fabric of his long sleeves—silk perhaps—on her throat. Through her lashes she could see only the coarse weave of the white cloth that covered her face.

He struggled with something and momentarily loosened his grip. In a last foolish effort to escape, she tried to go limp and squeeze out from under his stronghold.

He cursed and jerked her against him, the blade of the knife sharp against her neck, the stench of his cologne choking her. She felt the warm, sticky wetness of her own blood trickle down her chest. Light-headed and strangely calm now her thoughts were instantly clear as glass: *I'm going to die.*

The will to live was strong within her. Resisting would only hasten her death, and she forced herself to calm down, willed herself to stop struggling against the man's brute strength.

Anna had always imagined she would fight like a wildcat in a situation like this—fight to the death if necessary. She had a strong faith and did not fear death, but now the beautiful faces of Kara, Kassandra, and Paul—her sweet, sweet Paul—passed before her. And she knew at that moment she would submit to any horror if only she could live to see her family one more time.

"Please, God, help me! "She whispered a desperate prayer. "Oh, please don't let me die."

Anna fought to push what was happening from her mind. She felt herself being shoved to the ground, her clothing pushed and twisted immodestly. The gritty concrete ground into her back and hips. And then her abductor was on top of her, crushing her into the pavement. Fear and the heavy weight of his body paralyzed her, but with a sense of stunned astonishment, she realized she was living every woman's nightmare.

Please, God...

The crime she'd thought would never touch her was, in that very moment, becoming fact. She felt strangely detached from her own body, and despite the pain, she tried to sever herself from the horror, thinking only of surviving—for her daughters, for the man she loved.

A prayer swirled through her mind—one that seemed designed to distance her mind from what was happening to her. Even though the hood of cloth blinded her, she squeezed her eyes shut battling to stay conscious, despite being brutally violated.

Finally, the body atop her shuddered. He spat a vulgar oath, and she felt his weight lift as he crawled off of her.

She curled herself into a fetal position, tensing, praying he wouldn't take her life along with her dignity.

The heels of his shoes shuffled on the concrete kicking

fine sand in her face. She willed him to walk away. He took a staggering step, but then he turned, and spat in her still shrouded face. She turned her head away, resisting the instinct to rip off the saliva-soaked hood. If she saw his face, he would be more likely to kill her.

With a final vicious grunt, the man grabbed a hank of her hair and lifted her head by it, then he let go, and her head slammed onto the concrete.

She heard his footfalls running away and breathed out a strangled moan. Her whole head throbbed as she clambered blindly in the opposite direction. But when she tried to stand, everything swam

Mercifully, she tumbled into a black world of nothingness.

Three

Paul Marquette looked at his watch for the tenth time. The lobby of *Italia* was noisy and crowded and the hostess had already seated two parties in front of them. Where was Anna? He was sure they'd agreed on eight o'clock.

He tried her cell phone again. Straight to voicemail. He checked the time. Eight twenty-five. It wasn't like her to be late. At least not twenty-five minutes late. He'd seen her change her watch to Eastern time on the plane, and their cell phones had both synced automatically to local time, so he knew that wasn't her excuse.

Anna often turned her ringer off when she was in public places. She hated the rudeness cell phones had "perpetrated on society," as she put it, but surely by now she would have realized she was going to be late and tried to call. Maybe she'd lost her phone, but even then, she would have found a pay phone and called to let him know what was going on.

Had she gone back to the hotel and fallen asleep? Or slipped in the shower? Or— He didn't like where his thoughts were taking him. He called the hotel and asked them to ring the room. Again, no answer, but he left a message just in case.

Reluctantly, he allowed the waiter to seat him at a table near the entrance. He ordered a cup of coffee and an appetizer, but he was no longer hungry. He sipped the hot drink with one eye on the door. The waiter refilled his mug and brought a basket of breadsticks to the table, but he couldn't summon an appetite.

He dialed Anna's number every ten minutes, growing more frustrated by the minute. By nine o'clock he was genuinely alarmed. He put his head in his hands, raking his fingers through hair that had surely grown even grayer in the last hour. He had no clue where to begin looking for his wife in this sprawling city.

He called their hotel yet again and left another message. Then, leaving word with the restaurant hostess to detain Anna if she happened to show up there, he paid his bill and rose to leave.

He knew Anna had planned to do some shopping before dinner, so he hurried to their rental car and drove the short distance to Longwood Center. He parked near one of the main entrances and dashed to the front. He pushed hard on the door. Locked. Cupping his hands, he peered into the courtyard. He could see a maintenance crew sweeping the floor and some of the proprietors still securing the accordion gates that protected the storefronts. But the courtyard was devoid of shoppers. Anna couldn't be here.

He drove back to the restaurant, parked in the takeout lane, and ran inside. No luck. She hadn't shown up here either. Another quick call to the hotel proved fruitless. The concierge remembered a woman matching Anna's description leaving the hotel late in the afternoon after inquiring about whether Longwood Center was within walking distance, but the concierge hadn't seen her return and, of course, had no idea where she'd gone or with whom.

The knot in Paul's gut tightened. He didn't know where

else to turn. It was now nearly ten o'clock. He went back to the rental car and sat, tapping the steering wheel, trying to think what he should do next. In desperation, he dialed the Orlando Police.

He explained his situation to the officer that answered. "I've checked everyplace I can think of where she might possibly be. Can you tell me if any accidents have been reported, or... I don't know... What—what's next?" He felt almost embarrassed, like someone who'd carelessly lost a child.

"What did you say your name was again?"

"Marquette." He spelled the name out slowly, enunciating each letter.

"Mr. Marquette, chances are your wife just found a great sale at one of the malls. Does she know her way around the city?"

"No, not really. We've traveled here a couple times before, but..."

"Well, she may possibly have gotten lost. You're sure she wasn't confused about where you were to meet?"

"No, no. I'm certain she understood."

"What kind of vehicle was she driving?"

"She took a taxi from the hotel. She was on foot, but planned to take a cab to the restaurant, I'm sure."

"And she's not answering her phone?"

"No." Would he be calling the police if Anna was answering her phone? He bit back the sarcastic response. "Her phone goes straight to voicemail. I've called her fifty times in the last couple of hours." It wasn't much of an exaggeration.

"Well, I wouldn't be too worried at this point. Wouldn't be surprised if she's trying to call you right now. We get a lot of calls from worried husbands. Usually turns out to be nothing."

"No. You don't understand. Anna would never do something like this without calling to explain. She's just not like that."

"You didn't have a quarrel or anything, did you?" The

tone was condescending.

Furious with the officer's patronizing manner, Paul spoke through a clenched jaw. "No. Nothing like that."

"I'm sure she'll turn up." But the officer took down his information. "If you haven't located her by midnight, give us a call back, and we'll take the next step. Good luck, Mr. Marquette, and enjoy your stay in Orlando."

Paul heard the silence on the other end of the line, dismissing him. Maybe he should take comfort in the officer's assurance that it was likely all a misunderstanding, but he had a bad feeling about this. He clicked off his phone and turned the keys in the ignition. Reluctantly, he drove back to the hotel, checked in with the concierge, and when he was assured they had no new information, he stepped into the elevator.

He felt so helpless. Some instinct told him that his wife needed him desperately, yet he couldn't even find her. He jabbed at the buttons, struggling to think clearly, to even remember which floor they were staying on. The elevator stopped, and he squeezed between the doors before they had opened completely. He raced down the hall toward their room and hurriedly unlocked the door.

In the split second before he opened the door, he had a vivid vision of Anna sitting cross-legged on the bed, her beautiful smile lighting up the room as it always did, and her smooth blond hair, swinging and shiny, curving just below her chin. Throwing the door open, his heart sank seeing the emptiness of the room. But the neatly made beds and stacks of freshly folded towels confirmed she hadn't been here since they left the hotel this morning. His disappointment nearly took him to his knees.

He took a deep breath and forced himself to think. He had to stay calm if he was going to help her.

Sinking into a chair by the desk, he picked up the telephone, connected to an outside line, and dialed 911. He explained his situation as concisely as possible. The dispatcher started to put him through to the police department, but when he told her that he'd already contacted them, she connected him with the Orange County Sheriff's Office. They seemed to take his call more seriously than had the police officer he'd spoken to earlier. The deputy asked detailed questions, and Paul could hear a keyboard clicking as he took down the information Paul gave him. The deputy assured Paul that they would keep in touch and let him know if anything turned up.

He spent most of the night on the phone. He badgered the restaurant until finally he got no answer and assumed they'd closed. Then he called every agency in the city that he thought might possibly help. He also contacted every hospital in the Yellow Pages. In between, he checked his messages and forced himself to stay off the room phone in case Anna might be trying to reach him that way. He sat on the edge of the bed gripping his cell phone, staring at the room phone, willing one of them to ring.

Twice he started to dial Anna's parents. But each time he clicked off before it could ring on their end. He couldn't bear to worry them, and really, there was nothing they could do from halfway across the country.

He did call John Vickers, an account executive at Lindell and Bachman, the advertising firm where Paul had worked for the last decade. John and his wife, Brenda, had been close friends of the Marquettes ever since they'd found themselves seated across from each other at a company Christmas party eight years ago.

Brenda answered the phone.

"Hi, Brenda. It's Paul. I'm sorry for calling so late."

"Oh, no problem," she said cheerily. "We're still up. How are you?"

"I'm okay. Is John there?" Brenda was usually an obliging target of his teasing, but he hoped she could hear the urgency in his voice.

His curt reply evidently communicated the gravity of this call because Brenda seemed all business. "Just a minute. I'll get him."

Paul heard muffled voices, and then John was on the line. "Hi, Paul. I thought you were in Orlando."

"I am. Anna's missing, John."

"What?"

He explained the situation briefly, taking comfort in John's sympathetic murmurs. When he hung up a few minutes later, he knew that whatever could be done from that end, John would see that it was taken care of.

With great effort, Paul forced his lanky frame from the chair and trudged into the bathroom. He splashed warm water over his face and neck, then came out to sit on the bed, still clutching his cell phone, at a loss as to what he should do next. It was all he could do to restrain himself from running out into the night and searching every dark corner of the city single-handedly. But he knew that would be foolish—not to mention impossible—so he sat with his phone and prayed to God that his wife was safe and that this was all a terrible mix-up.

—ɯɯ—

The city's skyline had penciled itself against the coral Florida dawn when Paul finally put his head in his hands and wept in frustration and despair. He'd done everything he knew to do, and he was no closer to finding Anna than he'd been hours ago. He simply did not know where to turn next. The television in the hotel room droned softly in the background, tuned to a local news station in hopes there might be some clue offered there. There was plenty of news, none of it comforting.

"Please, God," he begged. Please…"

The urgent jangling of two phones—one next to the hotel bed and one on the desk—startled him as if it were an instant answer to his barely voiced prayer. He rubbed the fog from his eyes and looked at the clock. It was almost seven a.m.

The room was still dark, the morning light kept at bay by the heavy drapes drawn across the windows. Anna had been missing for over ten hours now.

The phone continued to ring, and Paul fumbled for the lamp switch, then picked up the receiver.

"Yes? Hello."

"Mr. Marquette?"

"Yes. What is it?" He sensed the urgency in the man's voice.

The caller identified himself as some liaison for an Orlando hospital. "Your wife is here. She's been injured…but she'll be fine," the man added quickly. "But you need to come right away."

"Oh, thank God." *Thank you, Lord.* "What happened? Is she okay? Can I speak to her?" His words caught on his emotion.

The caller assured Paul that Anna was out of danger and gave him detailed instructions to the hospital. Paul wrote the directions in cryptic scribblings on hotel stationery, but he didn't trust himself to drive there without getting lost—or getting a speeding ticket. So he called a cab and, closing the door behind him, dashed down the stairwell, too impatient to wait for the elevator to arrive.

Because of the Rain

Four

The taxi pulled up to the emergency entrance of the small hospital, and Paul jumped out. He thrust a twenty dollar bill through the window, not waiting for change. He raced through the double doors and down the corridor to the first desk he saw. Out of breath, he interrupted the nurses who stood there chatting.

"Please, my wife was admitted here—Anna Marquette. Do you know where she is?"

The two women looked at each other.

Paul was not comforted by what he saw in their faces. "Is she all right? What's happened?"

The older woman, plump and motherly, came around to where he stood. "Come with me, Mr. Marquette."

But instead of taking him to Anna, she led him to a small private waiting room—the kind of room they'd took him to when his father died on the operating table during open heart surgery. She ushered him to a chair by the window.

"Wait right here. The doctor will be in to speak with you

in just a few minutes." It was a command.

He sat down heavily, against his will, and sat there, unmoving, as the minutes crawled by. On the wall opposite him a standard issue institutional clock ticked off the seconds, each pulse reverberating in his head like a cannon. Strangely, no thoughts formed themselves in his mind. Time seemed suspended, waiting for this verdict.

Just after eight o'clock, Paul heard a door open somewhere and the hushed shuffling of shoes on carpet. Then a doctor stood over him, tall and imposing in his white coat. Paul struggled to his feet. At six foot three, he wasn't used to having others tower over him, but this man did.

"Mr. Marquette, I'm Dr. Blair." The physician extended his hand to Paul.

Paul took it, more to support his weight than to acknowledge the introduction. He opened his mouth to speak.

But the doctor held up a hand as if anticipating the questions. "Your wife is going to be fine. She's pretty beat up, and I don't think she's quite processed what happened yet, but she will recover."

Paul was confused. "What did happen?" In all the agonizing hours, wondering where Anna was, wondering what could have happened, the only thing he could fathom was that she'd been in an accident. Her cab had crashed, or she'd been hit by a car. What else could it be? And yet, this man spoke as though it were something more…something unspeakable.

The doctor looked stunned. "Oh, I'm sorry. I thought you knew."

Paul found his voice. "No one has told me anything."

The doctor grimaced and sat down in the chair Paul had just vacated. He motioned for Paul to take the seat beside him. Paul sat slowly, steeling himself.

"Mr. Marquette. There's no easy way to say this. Your wife was attacked, beaten, and raped." He gave the words a moment to sink in before continuing. "She's going to recover fully, but right now she's in pretty rough shape. Our biggest concern is that she may have a concussion. She has a nasty bump on the back of her head, and she was unconscious for several hours. That alone gives us reason for concern. In addition to that, her shoulder was dislocated, and she has a gash on her neck—a knife wound."

Paul must have gasped, for the doctor stretched out a hand and put it on his shoulder. "She's going to be okay," he assured. "The cut looks pretty wicked, but actually it isn't very deep. It didn't require stitches, and it should heal with a minimum of scarring." He paused. "Your wife is lucky to be alive, Mr. Marquette."

"Did they...did they catch whoever did this?"

"Let's worry about your wife right now. As I'm sure you can imagine, sexual assault is one of the most traumatic things a woman can endure. Your wife is still somewhat in shock right now. This will take some time to process. I'm not sure she even quite realizes what has happened."

Paul's head was spinning. He had so many questions he didn't know where to start, but they all came tumbling out, one after another.

"Who...who found her? Where was she? Where is she now?"

The doctor answered him calmly. "I'll take you to her very shortly. She was found in an alley behind Longwood Center—it's a big shopping mall near the convention center. I believe it was a sanitation worker who found her there sometime after midnight. The ambulance brought her in"—he referred to the folder in his hands—"it says here 1:15 a.m. I first examined her around 1:45. She was unconscious when they found her, but she regained consciousness in the ambulance. We knew from the identification in her purse that she was a nonresident, but for obvious reasons, there was no answer at your home number when one of the nurses called. Your wife's cell phone was damaged—broken—and she couldn't remember where you were staying here in Orlando, so her hotel key was turned over to the police for an identification search. Of course, the police knew she'd been reported missing. That's how we were able to locate you."

Paul sat stiff, nodding numbly at this assault of information, trying to piece the story together. It concerned him that Anna hadn't been able to remember where they were staying.

"From what we can gather," the doctor continued, "your wife didn't get a look at her attacker. Perhaps she'll be able to tell us more as she recovers and starts to remember some details. Right now we don't want to upset her any more than is absolutely necessary. We've done the preliminary examination, but we need to run some more tests. I want to make sure there aren't any internal injuries, and we'll want to take precautions in case she was exposed to any sexually transmitted diseases or other infections." He rose slowly from the chair and turned to Paul, smiling sympathetically. "The best thing we can do for her now is to get you in to see her. She's been asking for you since she regained consciousness."

Dr. Blair strode briskly down the emergency room corridor. Paul followed a few steps behind. He was trembling with a strange mingling of relief and anger and paralyzing fear.

Dr. Blair stopped abruptly before a door that stood slightly ajar. He tapped lightly before entering, and when he stepped aside, holding the door open for Paul, there was Anna. Paul knew it was her, because her flaxen hair was spread on the pillow beneath her head. But the face that went with the slight form on the bed was unrecognizable as his Anna. Dark bluish circles ringed her eyes. Her face was blotchy and swollen. Her neck was swathed in white gauze almost to her chin, and her left arm, resting on the hospital blankets, lay limp in a sling. Her eyes were closed, but somehow Paul knew she was not asleep.

Involuntarily, he put his fist to his mouth, stifling a gasp. Struggling to collect himself, he went to her bedside and took her right hand in his. The faint scent of her perfume mingled with the antiseptic odors of the room.

Paul kissed her hand and whispered her name.

Her eyes flickered open, then widened when she recognized him. She lifted her head off the pillows but winced in pain and fell back onto the bed. She tried to speak, but words would not come—only tears that flowed freely, dampening her hair as they rolled off her temples.

Finally she formed the words. "I'm sorry I was late."

It took Herculean effort for him not to scoop her into his arms and crush her to himself. Instead he took her wounded head carefully between his large hands. With his thumbs, he wiped the tears away and gently stroked her hair away from her face.

"Oh, Anna... Honey, I'm so sorry. I... I should have been there. I should never have let this happen. I should have been with you." He heard anger rise in his own voice and stopped speaking lest she think his ire was directed at her.

Wordlessly, he cradled her head, taking in every bruise, every bump, every mark that marred her beautiful skin. He searched her blue-gray eyes for assurance that she truly was going to be all right. Then he silently gave thanks that she was here in this place of healing, still alive, still his. And he cursed the monster who had done this to his wife.

Anna sighed heavily and closed her eyes again. For the next hour she drifted in and out of sleep. Paul sat beside her bed, watching as she intermittently opened her eyes, searched the room until she found him, then, with a look of relief washing across her face, closed her eyes again.

A nurse came, followed by two aides, and explained to them that it was time to move Anna to another examination room. They lifted her onto a gurney and wheeled her down the crowded hallway and into a sterile room a few doors down. Paul followed. Dr. Blair came into the room and quietly explained that they had been so concerned with the treatment of Anna's neck wound, her shoulder, and the concussion that the rape itself had been the least of their immediate worries. Now they needed to examine her to determine if there was any serious internal damage from the assault. The hospital utilized a rape kit that would test for infection, disease, and existing pregnancy, as well as collect any evidence that might still remain.

Anna was offered the morning-after pill, which she quickly declined. "I'd really recommend it," the nurse said. "There are usually no serious side effects if you're not pregnant, but it will take care of things quickly and easily if by some horrible odds you are."

But the whole time the nurse was speaking, Anna was shaking her head vehemently.

"It really is a precaution we recommend." The nurse persisted.

"No," Paul spoke for Anna, trying to put the possibility out of his mind. "She's said no. That's all."

The nurse clucked her disapproval, but Dr. Blair seemed to give her a silent sign.

The doctor turned to Paul and asked if they wanted to report the rape. "You don't have to make that decision right now, but because of the violent nature of the attack, we strongly recommend that you do report it. Depending on the circumstances, you can always drop the charges later, but the sooner it's reported, and the more evidence we can collect, the better the chances of finding and prosecuting her attacker."

Anna's eyes went wide. "Prosecute? Do they know who did it?"

"No," the doctor admitted. "Hopefully the police are close to finding—"

"No." The strength in Anna's voice encouraged Paul.

"I don't want to drag this out," she said.

"I understand, and you should take some time to think this through," Dr. Blair said. "But if you do decide to report it, it's good to have photos as evidence—of the brutality of the attack. Would you object if we took some pictures...of the bruises and bandages?"

"No! No pictures! Paul...?" She turned toward him, but the sudden movement caused her to moan in pain.

He held up a hand to quiet her. He was frankly surprised by her adamant refusal. But he would understood how humiliating this must feel. Anna had always been a very private person.

He would support her wishes. He turned to Dr. Blair. "No pictures," he said firmly.

—m—

As Anna lay vulnerable on the hard examination table, memories of her ordeal seeped back into her mind, stinging like alcohol in a raw wound. The doctor aimed a bright light beneath the sheet that draped her legs and Anna saw in her mind the coarse weave of the cloth that had covered her face last night. She felt she might suffocate.

She despised her nakedness beneath the thin hospital gown and tried to wave Paul out of the room. But he shushed her and stood firmly planted beside the table where she lay. He held her gaze, forcing her to look into his eyes. He smoothed her forehead with gentle hands, and she winced, not in pain but in humiliation. Paul closed her eyes gently with his fingers and let his large warm hands rest lightly on her forehead, covering her eyes with the palm of his hand as though he could take away her self-imposed shame by sparing her his scrutiny. She loved him all the more for the act.

When the examination was finished, a nurse drew two vials of blood from her arm, explaining that it would be several days before any of the test results would be available. She was given an antibiotic—"to be on the safe side," the nurse said—then wheeled down the hallway, into an elevator, and on to the private room Paul had requested.

Paul followed the orderly, hovering over Anna. Dr. Blair informed them he wanted her to stay at least overnight so that her head injury could be monitored closely. "I'll make rounds late tomorrow morning when I get out of surgery," Dr. Blair said. "We can decide then about making the trip back to Chicago.

The nurses came in to check Anna's vital signs and get her settled in the room. Paul searched her face, and she forced a smile for his sake.

He leaned over and kissed the tip of her nose. "I think I'm in the way here," he said, motioning toward the nurses. "I'm going to step out into the hall for a few minutes. You'll be all right?"

Anna nodded, feeling groggy.

Walking into the hallway, Paul looked both directions down the corridor. A sign on the left pointed to a waiting room. Blindly he followed the arrows. His thoughts churned incomprehensibly. He simply could not grasp everything he'd learned in the past hour. He fought to stay in control. He had to find a place where he could be alone.

The arrows led him to a large, empty waiting room. Vinyl-covered chairs lined three walls, and a dusty television peered out over the room from its metal shelf in a corner near the ceiling. The TV was tuned to a soap opera, but the volume was turned low so that the actors' dramatic expressions, without the dialogue, were strangely comical. A row of large windows stretched down one wall of the room. The opposite wall was rough hewn brick, empty of chairs or any decoration save plastic lettering that spelled out *William C. Dreiling Memorial Wing*. Paul gazed aimlessly out the windows onto the parking lot below.

His mind reeled as he realized how close he'd been to Anna last night while she lay bleeding and helpless in that alley. A horrible knowledge came to him: while he'd sat in a restaurant sipping coffee, lounging in comfort, Anna had been suffering the most brutal violation imaginable. She'd needed him as never before, and he had failed her. In fact, he'd been angry with her because he thought she was late. He should have known better. It wasn't like Anna to be late. He'd told the police officer that, but the man had brushed him off. "But I should have insisted," Paul berated himself. "I should have known something was wrong. I should have known!"

A memory, a fragment of a conversation he'd had with Anna years before, came to Paul. He hadn't thought of it since the day it had occurred many years ago. At the time, it was of no consequence. Now it haunted him. When he and Anna were dating, a string of rapes had plagued the neighborhood where Anna was teaching school. She'd become frightened and fearful of walking to school alone. Paul had teased her and discounted her fears, but he did agree to walk her to and from work each day, and he'd bragged overconfidently that nothing could happen to her as long as she had him to protect her. Now he felt sick at his cocky boasting. Where had he been last night? Where had he been the one time she desperately needed his protection? What kind of a man was he?

He'd never felt so powerless or so full of rage as he did at this moment. His head felt as though it would explode. He paced back and forth between the windows and the empty brick wall across the room. Fury rose in waves within him, until abruptly, he turned and pounded his fists on the brick wall, beating his knuckles against the rough surface until they bled. His mouth opened in a howl of anguish, but no sound came forth. Finally spent, he sunk into the cold upholstery of a waiting room chair and put his head in his hands.

He sat that way until he felt blood from his scraped fingers trickle slowly toward his wrists. The warm wetness startled him, and he held his hands in front of his face as though he couldn't remember how the wounds had come to be there. He rose slowly, holding his hands aloft like a freshly scrubbed surgeon, taking care not to get blood on his clothes. He found a rest room and washed his hands, holding them under the cool running water for several minutes. Then blotting the wounds with paper towels, he walked to the nurse's station and, embarrassed, asked for a few bandages.

"Good grief! What did you do?" asked a young nurse,

vigorously chewing a wad of gum. She didn't look a day over sixteen.

"It's nothing," Paul told her. "I'm okay. I just need a couple of Band-Aids, please."

"Don't you want to put something on that? Looks pretty nasty."

Paul waved her away. "No, no. It's all right. Just Band-Aids. Please."

Reluctantly the nurse handed him a stack of large sterile bandages, and he went back to the restroom and applied them clumsily to each bleeding knuckle.

When he got back to Anna's room, she was sleeping. A large uncomfortable-looking lounge chair sat between the window and Anna's bed. Paul eased himself into the chair's awkward embrace and tried to doze off.

It was no use. Too many thoughts fought for his attention. He sat up and, perching on the edge of the chair, watched his wife sleep. He let his gaze travel from her tousled head, past the bandages that swathed her neck, down to her hands that lay upon the white sheets. His eyes rested on the simple diamond that she wore on her left hand. Anna's hands were delicate and expressive, her nails always carefully manicured. How he loved those hands. And how privileged he felt that this woman wore his wedding ring. *Oh, Anna. How could anyone have done this to you?* His Anna, who was only sweetness and light, who would never have hurt anyone. How could he have let this happen? *How?* He leaned his head against the cold metal rail of her bed and wept silently.

Five

Anna had been given a sedative and slept most of the afternoon. Around three o'clock Paul went to the hospital's small cafeteria and bought a cup of coffee and a Danish. It was the first thing he had eaten since the appetizer he'd nibbled on at *Italia* the night before. He really wasn't hungry, but he knew he needed to keep up his strength.

He also needed to call his daughters. He would give any-thing—absolutely anything—if he could just pretend this never happened. But it *had* happened, and Kara and Kassi would never forgive him if he didn't call them today.

He found a relatively quiet hallway and dialed Kara's number. Their older daughter had an apartment in Urbana, but she was hard to catch. She was studying veterinary medicine and worked every spare hour at an animal clinic near the university, and rarely had her phone turned on. He let it ring a dozen times, counting each unanswered burr aloud. When it finally went to voice mail, he left a terse message, then fished in his wallet for the number at the clinic.

Kara herself answered on the second ring, her voice soft and cheerful. He hated that he was about to break her heart. "Meadowbrook Animal Clinic. This is Kara. May I help you?"

His little girl sounded so grown up, so professional. He could almost see her now, her white blond hair pulled into a ponytail, her blue eyes bright and inquisitive, a white lab coat over faded jeans.

"Hi, Kara." He tried to warn her by the tone of his greeting that this wasn't a casual call.

"Dad?" A pause. "Is everything okay? I thought you were in Florida."

"We are, honey. We've had...some problems. Your mom is in the hospital."

"Oh, Dad! What happened?"

"Sit down, Kara." He could hear her start to cry, and he hurried to finish his story. "Honey, Mom was assaulted last night. She's going to be okay but she was hurt pretty badly. The guy...um, the guy raped her and cut her throat..." He broke down, saying these terrible words out loud. But Kara's gasp and her bitter sobs sobered him, and he went on, suddenly strong for his daughter's sake.

"The cut isn't deep, honey. It's not as bad as it sounds." He winced. Why had he told her about the knife wound? It would only worry her more. He hurried on. "Kara, Mom's going to be okay. Really. And she's taking it very well. She's... she's holding up very well," he repeated. "But, honey, Mom's going to need our help." He told his daughter the details he knew, assuring her with each part of the story that Anna would recover, that she was all right.

Kara voiced a new thought. "Dad, does Kassi know?"

"No, honey. I haven't called her yet."

Kara's tears started afresh. "Poor Kassi. She'll take this so hard."

Kara was right. Kassi was the tenderhearted one. Kara was stubborn and independent and as strong as they came. She'd be fine. But he was worried about his younger daughter.

Kassi was at Illinois State in Bloomington. Her first year away from home had been tough, and she'd almost decided not to go back after Christmas break. But reason had won out, and second semester was going much more smoothly for her. Now he had to give her this awful news.

"Dad, please let me tell her," Kara pleaded now. "I'll drive up tonight and bring her back to my apartment. We could fly to Orlando first thing in the morning, if I can get reservations that quickly."

"No, don't do that, Kara. I really think we'll come home sometime tomorrow. They just want to keep Mom overnight as a precaution. The doctor is supposed to see her late tomorrow morning, and I guess we'll know for sure then. But I would *appreciate* it if you would tell Kassi. She'll need someone with her. Why don't you girls stay at your place, and I'll call you there as soon as I know something."

"Well, okay. Are you sure you don't want us to come?"

"I'm sure, but thanks for offering, honey." He gave her Anna's room number at the hospital and hung up, grateful that task was over, and thankful Kassi wouldn't have to be alone when she heard the news. How it would have comforted him to wrap his daughters in his arms right now.

Feeling somewhat relieved, he walked back down to Anna's room and found her sitting up in bed trying to sip ice water from a straw. He went to her side and held the glass for her. Above the bandages she gave him a crooked smile, and he felt his spirits lift for the first time since last night.

She took one last sip and motioned that she'd had enough. Paul set the glass on her bedside tray and took Anna's hands in his.

"I called Kara."

"Oh, Paul. Did you have to?"

"Anna, you know I did."

She sighed. "I know. But... I wish the girls didn't have to deal with this."

"That wouldn't be fair."

She nodded in resigned agreement. When he tightened his grasp on her hands, she looked down and for the first time noticed the bandages on his knuckles.

"Paul! What did you do to your hand? Both of them! What happened, honey?"

He pulled his hands away and mumbled, "Nothing. It's nothing. I'm fine." How like Anna to lie there, beaten within an inch of her life, and worry about *his* little scrapes. Love for her filled his heart and threatened to spill over in tears. He quickly changed the subject.

"Kara is going to drive up and get Kassi and let her know what's going on. They'll stay at Kara's tonight." He paused and then said tenderly, "Anna, I know you don't want to talk about it, but I think we need to report this to the police. That guy is still out there somewhere..." He let his voice trail off and waited for her response. She was silent.

Gently he posed the question. "What do you remember about it, honey? I know this isn't easy for you, but it's important. Do you know what he looked like?"

"Paul, I don't remember hardly anything. I know he"— she started crying—"I know he raped me. Oh, Paul, he raped me. Can you ever forgive me?"

"Anna, forgive you for *what*?" He was incredulous.

"It was so stupid of me to go out that way. I don't know what I was thinking. I should have known better. I should have fought harder."

"Anna, how could you know?" He took her chin between his thumb and forefinger and forced her to look at him. "This was not your fault, Anna. I don't want to hear you talk like that again." He was stern and truly angry with her for being so irrational. It emboldened him to ask the hard questions. "Tell me what you do remember. What did he look like?"

She closed her eyes and cringed, but he could tell she was working to remember, if only to help them find this monster.

"I remember he put something over my head...some kind of bag or... or cloth. I never saw his face, Paul. I never saw him..." She sounded perplexed at the realization. "But I remember his voice. He... he had an accent. European...like French, or something, I think. Yes, he called me mademoiselle. I remember that." She spoke quickly now as the memories came back to her in a rush.

"I told him to take my money, and he... he said it wasn't money he was after. I tried to fight him, Paul. Honest, I did try to fight him. But then he... he cut me. He had a knife... oh, he had a knife ..." Fighting tears, she put her free hand to her neck almost involuntarily. Her voice trailed off, and it was as though she were speaking to herself now.

"Strange, it... it really didn't hurt. Not then. But I could feel the blood, and I thought he was going to kill me. Oh, Paul... I thought... I thought I was going to die. After he ..." She began to weep, her fist to her mouth. "After he was done, he shoved me, and... I... I don't remember anything else until the ambulance. Oh. I think he was tall. I remember his voice was way above me. I don't know just how tall, but taller than you, I think." She lurched forward, begging him. "Paul, do we have to report this? I don't want everybody to have to know this happened. I just want to go home. I want to forget about it. Please, Paul?" Her voice was pleading.

"Anna, of course I won't make you report it. But I don't think it's right to just forget it. Think of Kara and Kassi. If this had happened in Chicago, wouldn't you want that guy locked away?" He knew he'd hit a soft spot. He felt guilty coercing her, but he thought the situation warranted it. And he wanted that lousy excuse for a human being put away forever.

Reluctantly Anna agreed, and before she could change her mind, Paul asked the hospital to notify the police.

They were eating supper in Anna's room when an officer knocked at the door. He quickly put Anna at ease with his fatherly manner and gently coaxed her to tell him the details of her assault.

Strange. This time yesterday, Anna had been happily shopping, and Paul had just been seated in the restaurant, eagerly waiting to tell his wife about his meetings and to find out what she'd done with her day. Now he would do anything to turn back the clock.

Paul had played the scene over and over in his mind: Anna being brutally attacked, then lying helpless and bleeding in that alley just steps away from where he'd been. Just steps away! He was supposed to be Anna's protector, and he'd impatiently sipped coffee while she bled. He'd beaten himself up for that. He had awakened from brief catnaps, arms flailing the air in front of him, trying to atone in his dreams for his failure to protect the woman he loved. He wasn't sure he would ever come to terms with his monstrous failure. It almost made it worse that Anna had so completely forgiven him—in fact, had never accused him in the first place. He didn't deserve her. And yet, how grateful he was that she belonged to him, that she was here in the safety of this hospital, and that she was alive.

The nurses came in and helped Anna get up to use the bathroom. They carefully dressed her wounds and helped her wash her face and get settled in bed again.

When they left, Paul kissed her good-night and sank into the big chair near her bed. This time he knew he would sleep.

Six

Paul awoke to the sound of the breakfast carts rumbling out of the elevators in the hallway and the hushed voices of the nurses changing shifts. Rubbing his neck, he stood up, testing his muscles. His whole body ached from sleeping in the chair. He'd slept so soundly that he didn't think he'd changed positions once, but the stiffness was a small price to pay for the much needed rest.

He saw Anna's form, dwarfed in the imposing hospital bed, and slowly he began to remember the events of the previous day. He watched her chest rise and fall until he was convinced that she was breathing easily, and then he went into the room's small lavatory to wash his face and bring some order to his tousled hair.

Anna stirred when she heard Paul emerge from the bathroom. She tried to sit up in the bed, but intense pain seared through her shoulder and pounded in her head. She felt the wound on her neck pull and tighten. Groaning, she lay back against the firm pillows.

Paul toyed with the remote control until he found the buttons that raised the head of the bed. Wordlessly, he helped her swing her legs over the side. She perched on the edge of the bed, catching her breath and testing the pain before she tried to stand.

She'd walked to the bathroom the night before with a nurse on either side. Now she did so with only Paul's arm for support. She tested her legs gingerly, and when she decided she felt strong, she dismissed him with a wave of her sling, clutching the immodest hospital gown to a close in back with her free hand.

Anna wrestled with the tough plastic wrapping on the new toothbrush the hospital had provided. Her frustrated grumblings brought Paul back into the bathroom. He opened the package and squeezed a stripe of toothpaste on the brush. He handed it to Anna with a flourish, and she began to brush her teeth vigorously.

"Do you have everything you need now, honey?" he asked.

"Uh-huh," she mumbled through a mouthful of toothpaste. She gargled and spat noisily into the sink.

"Okay. I'm going to head down to the nurses' station and see if I can find out when the doctor will be making rounds. Be back in a minute."

She waved him away.

Anna peered into the mirror in the dimly lit bathroom. Oh, she looked awful! Like death warmed over, her mother would have said. It felt good to wash her face and brush her teeth, but oh, how desperately she wanted a bath. She longed to soak away the grime of the alley that she imagined imbedded in her back. She wanted to scrub the place where he had gripped her arm so tightly. And though her neck was tender and sore, she wanted to wash it, too, to banish every contamination that he'd inflicted on her. Mostly, she wanted to wash away the memory of the whole sordid ordeal. She wanted to pretend that she was here in this hospital because she had a simple virus. She desperately needed to be well and to walk out of here and get on an airplane and go home. Then she wanted to pretend that none of it had ever happened.

Maybe she could have, if no one else had known. But Paul knew. Her daughters knew. And seemingly every law enforcement agency in Florida knew. So she would have to acknowledge that it had happened. She would have to sort it out with everyone watching carefully to see how she was doing when they didn't think she was looking, to see if she was going to fall apart or if she was going to go on living.

Anna walked with halting steps back to the nightstand by her bed and rummaged through the drawer of toiletries the hospital had supplied. She found a flimsy comb and went back to the bathroom mirror and began to work out the knots in her hair.

The pale fine hair around her temples and at the nape of her neck was matted with flecks of dried blood and was hopelessly tangled. She dampened the comb and worked out a snarl, wincing in pain, but determined to finish the task before she retreated to the refuge of the hospital bed.

She stood there, lost in thought, painstakingly working on a section of hair at a time. From the corner of her eye, a shadowy figure flitted behind her reflection in the mirror. Anna's heart stopped beating. She whirled around, panic-stricken. The raw terror she'd felt in the grasp of that monster revisited her, and she broke out in a cold sweat. A sob of relief escaped her lips when she realized it was Paul standing in the doorway, oblivious to the fear he'd innocently caused her. She fell against him, unable to explain to him this awful panic that held her in its grip.

At ten o'clock, Anna's doctor stepped into her room and briefly examined her. He tucked the stethoscope into the pocket of his lab coat and looked at her over the top of smudged reading glasses. "Well, you've been through quite an ordeal, Mrs. Marquette, but I have no problem dismissing you today, if you feel well enough to leave. It looks like the concussion was relatively mild. I don't think it will pose an ongoing problem." He looked at her chart. "Let's see, home is Chicago?"

Husband and wife nodded in unison.

"You are flying, I assume? I'm not sure how you'll feel about making a trip right away. You may want to go back to your hotel and rest for a couple of days before you tackle the airways. But I'll leave that up to you. If you feel up to it, there's certainly no reason why you couldn't fly, even as early as this afternoon." With those words, the doctor smiled reassuringly at Anna, shook Paul's hand, and left the room.

The nurse on duty gave Anna instructions for dressing the wound on her neck and caring for her shoulder. Then she gave her a thick stack of pamphlets with titles like "Sexual Assault: How to Cope" and "Help for Victims of Rape," explaining gently that she might find them helpful. Anna stuffed them into the drawer of the nightstand beside her bed, embarrassed to have them lying out in the open where anyone might see them.

When the nurse had gone, Anna turned to Paul and pleaded, "Please, honey, let's go home. I just want to get out of here."

"Anna, are you sure you don't want to stay at the hotel for a few days?"

"No!" She was vehement. "I want to go home, Paul. I know I can make it. Couldn't you get our tickets changed?"

"I'm sure I can arrange something if you're positive that's what you want to do." He looked skeptical.

"I'm sure."

Paul signed the papers that released Anna from the hospital's responsibility and left to make arrangements for changing their flight and canceling his meetings.

Anna lay in the hospital bed, not moving. She stared out the window at Orlando's skyline. And the thought played over and over through her mind, "If only I can get away from this city—back home to Chicago—if only I can go home, I think I can make it."

The airport was crowded with students returning from spring break, and their noisy revelry pounded in Anna's head. Paul helped her find an empty seat near the ticket counter. He herded their luggage through the snaking line that ended at the baggage check-in, sending Anna a reassuring smile each time the line moved forward a few inches.

She looked awful. Although the nurses had helped her with a hurried shower before she left the hospital, Anna had not been able to shampoo her hair, and now it hung in limp strands around her face. Her eyes were puffy and ringed with mottled green-and-purple circles. The bandages on her neck stood out like a beacon above her scoop-necked top, drawing stares from everyone who passed within a few feet of her chair. Anna was acutely aware of the furtive glances and the pointing and whispering. She hadn't thought of this when she'd begged Paul to let her fly home today. She pulled her light jacket close around her, but it did little to camouflage the gauzy scarf of a bandage wound around her neck.

Closing her eyes, Anna rested her head on her hand, her thoughts slipping back, against her will, to the horror of the attack. The heavy sigh of someone settling into the seat beside her brought Anna back to the present, but she kept her eyes closed, hoping to avoid an awkward encounter.

But the large woman who had just taken up residence next to her was not to be deterred. She put her hand heavily on Anna's arm and spoke in a booming voice that grated harshly on Anna's fragile nerves.

"Good grief, sweetheart. What happened to you? Looks like you got hit by a Mack truck." She howled at her own joke, and Anna was forced to look at her.

She gave the older woman a wan smile, hoping that would satisfy her, but the woman was undaunted. She leaned toward Anna and eyed her wounds more closely. Then in a loud, conspiratorial stage whisper, she asked, "Did your man work you over, honey? Hey, listen, I've been there. Believe me, I know what you're going through. Leave the fool, I say. That's what I did…"

Horrified, Anna held up her hand to silence the woman's misplaced harangue. "No, no! It's not like that! I… I got, uh…I was mugged in the city, that's all." Before she could stop them, tears welled in her eyes. She turned away, but the woman persisted.

"Oh my! What is this world coming to? Well, it looks like you fought like a barracuda! Did he get your money?"

"He…no, he didn't get…" Anna was beginning to panic. She looked around desperately for Paul, but the line had moved again, and Paul was at the far end of the queue with his back toward Anna. Their carry-on luggage was at her feet. She didn't think she could move it all herself, but she was frantic to escape this interrogation.

Mercifully, the woman's traveling companion, a younger version of herself, had finished checking their luggage and came over to escort her mother to the concourse. Anna sighed and willed Paul to hurry.

Finally their bags were checked, and Paul guided her protectively through the terminal. Anna felt weak and exhausted, and by the time they reached their departure gate, she almost wished she had accepted Paul's offer of finding a wheelchair for her. They were able to board immediately, and he helped her get settled in a window seat. He sat forward, shielding her from the questioning glances of the passengers who filed down the aisle, checking seat numbers and stowing coats and baggage.

Aside from the stares and whispers, the rest of the flight home was uneventful. After a short stopover in St. Louis, they were airborne to Chicago. Anna began to feel the relief of being almost home.

As their plane taxied smoothly along the runway at O'Hare, Anna felt a sense of well-being and serenity wash over her. She was home. She was safe. *She was alive!*

Kara and Kassi had been waiting at O'Hare since an hour

before the flight was scheduled to arrive. Anna watched her daughters' worried frowns turn into teary smiles of relief as they spotted their parents making their way down the ramp. Anna walked out into the waiting area on Paul's arm and was swept immediately into the embraces of her daughters. They exclaimed over her bruises and bandages. They fawned over her until she was worn out by their attention. But no mention was made of the rape or any part of the attack, and for now, Anna was content to leave it that way. She was grateful for their sweet solicitousness. But in the back of her mind, she knew she would have to talk about it. Her daughters would want to know the details of what had happened. And she would have to face the reality of what had happened to her. She *needed* to talk about it.

After the hours of trauma and wakefulness, Anna fell asleep easily that night—happy to have the girls in their old rooms and Paul's arms wrapped gently around her, taking such tender care not to hold too tightly where she was bruised and bandaged.

At 2:30 a.m., she awoke with a start. Her heart was thumping in her chest, and she was drenched in perspiration. It took her a moment to remember that she was back home, but as the memories pushed their way back into her consciousness, she knew why she was so shaken.

She'd dreamed about *him*. He was chasing her down a black alley. In her dream the smothering white shroud covered *his* head as he towered over her. She tried to run, but her legs were leaden. He came closer, closer, and she seemed to lose ground with every labored step.

As much as she didn't want to have a face to put on her attacker, it was almost worse not knowing. Because now, he could be *any* man.

Fully awake now, Anna watched the digital clock on her bedside table turn to three o'clock and then four. A hundred times she replayed the scene in her mind. Only now it was not the dream. She saw herself just as she'd been that night in Orlando—walking around the outside of the mall. She remembered the sleeveless blue dress she'd been wearing, even the pale pink nail polish she'd applied that morning in the hotel. They'd apparently removed it in the hospital, but now she remembered its shimmering color clearly. She felt the weight of the shopping bags she'd carried and then felt the sharp blow to her shoulder.

Slowly, agonizingly, she remembered every detail of the attack. The struggle, his harsh words, the sickening accent he'd spoken in. She wasn't sure now if it was real or affected.

When she finally came to the end of her memories, where she'd lost consciousness, she began all over again. With each remembrance, each private telling of the story, some small detail that had lain dormant until this moment came clearly into focus. He'd cursed at her. A filthy word she only heard in R-rated movies. The man had spit in her face, too.

It all seemed so unbelievable that somehow she had to make it real in her mind, because it had happened to her. It was true, and the more she relived it, the more it became truth for her.

And when she tired of replaying the attack in her mind, she began what she came to think of as the what ifs. *What if I had chosen another exit from the mall? What if I had taken a taxi instead of walking? What if I had left a few minutes earlier or a few minutes later?* She tortured herself with these questions, always coming back to reality. What ifs meant nothing. If onlys served no purpose. It had happened to her just the way it did. Now she had to accept that and live with it.

The numbers on the digital clock flashed to four-thirty, and still she'd not been able to quiet her thoughts. She sat up in bed and swung her legs over the side. The room was dark and a half moon cast eerie shadows on the walls. Paul snored softly on his side of the bed. Without turning on the lamp on her nightstand, Anna stood unsteadily in the darkness and groped her way to the door. A night-light glowed from an outlet in the hallway and Anna edged toward the bathroom, feeling her way along the wall with her uninjured arm.

Irrationally, her heart began to pound with fear. Never before had she been afraid in her own house. Even when Paul was traveling, she'd always felt safe here. She forced herself to keep going, moving cautiously down the hallway. Finally, she reached the open doorway and grasped the doorframe to orient herself.

Trembling, she switched on the bathroom light and closed the door softly, locking it behind her. She unwound the gauze bandage from her neck and dropped it into the wastebasket. She examined her face in the mirror, looking past the bruises, the scrapes, the gash on her neck and into the eyes of a woman who had been brutalized and raped.

Did she know this woman? Would she ever feel like herself again? Would her life ever be the same?

She stood for long minutes looking at her reflection. *I was raped.* Feeling silly, she mouthed the words at her reflection. *I was raped.* In despair, she slid to the floor and sat beside the bathtub with her back to the wall. She'd thought that coming home—to Chicago, to this house—would be her healing. She should be grateful for her very life. And she was. *Oh, Lord…it could have been so much worse.*

Great heaving sobs wracked her weakened body. She let them come, and finally she stood and turned on the faucet and began to fill the bathtub with water. She slipped off her nightgown and stepped into the tub, cringing at the scalding water. She lathered the washcloth and scrubbed her body until her skin was raw. Then she pulled the plug and watched the water run out of the tub, imagining the filth of her attack draining into the sewer where it belonged. She turned on the shower and stood and let the clean hot water rinse her body. Then she stepped out of the tub, dried off, and put her nightgown back on.

She turned to open the door. The familiar fear gripped her once more. Suddenly, she was terrified of what might be on the other side of the door. The hallway would be dark. Her eyes would not be adjusted to the blackness. She would be vulnerable, alone. What *if he* was out there? One part of her knew she was being irrational, and yet she could not still the quaking of her heart in her chest. She took a ragged breath and, shivering, opened the door. She left the bathroom light on to illuminate her path down the hallway and hurried back to their room.

She slipped into the warmth of the bed, careful not to awaken her husband. Paul's even breathing was a comfort, and Anna reached out to put her hand lightly against his back, wanting just to touch him, to find security in his warmth, in his presence. Finally, she closed her eyes and slept deeply, until the blare of the alarm clock roused them both at seven.

It was a ritual that repeated itself every night for a week: the dream, the awakening, the scene playing over and over and over in her mind, the tiptoeing into the bathroom for the release of tears, the cleansing bath, and finally the trip back to bed where slumber overtook her. It was a catharsis. For a while at least, she felt purged of the horror of what had happened to her. And always after the tears, she slept deeply beside Paul until the sun fell across their pillows.

Seven

The week ended, and still none of them had broached the subject of the rape. Kara tended her mother's physical wounds, joking that she'd had plenty of practice on the dogs and cats at the clinic.

Anna relished her eldest daughter's devoted attention.

Her relationship with their firstborn had seemed fragile almost from the moment the girl had been born. Kara was headstrong and opinionated, qualities that had served her well when it came to resisting peer pressure and standing up for her beliefs, but which made parenting her a challenge that often utterly exhausted Anna.

A young woman of many talents and something of a perfectionist, Kara would not have dared to risk her future in the types of rebellion that most parents feared—experimenting with alcohol, drugs, sex. Quite the contrary, she was an excellent student, a model citizen. But she chafed at any parental limits set for her, and until the day she left home, she had challenged her mother's authority at every turn. The friction between mother and daughter was heightened by the fact that Kara adored her father.

When Kara left for college, she and Anna had struck a tenuous unspoken truce, and now Anna was grateful for the absence of the usual tension between them.

Kassandra, on the other hand, had inherited her father's compliant, carefree spirit, and it showed itself now as she helped her mother with the practical things. She kept the laundry done and cleaned the already immaculate house until it sparkled.

When Paul got home from work each day that first week, he greeted Anna with a careful hug and asked the same question with his usual sweet sincere concern: "How are you doing, hon?"

But his question was rife with ambiguity. The tenderness in his voice spoke volumes, and he held her in his arms in bed each night until she slept, something he hadn't ordinarily done before the attack. But despite his gentleness, they couldn't seem to get past the superficial.

How *was* she doing? Her wounds were healing. Life was resuming its routine. But the real wounds weren't so easily dressed and healed. *Her heart hurt.* The real issues remained buried in a pile of guilt and uncertainty and fear. Anna had been raped. *Raped!*

And because Anna so completely belonged to Paul, he too had been violated.

Paul didn't quite know what to make of the feelings of jealousy—rage even—that he was entertaining. Intellectually, he knew that Anna had not betrayed him. Quite the opposite. If there was a betrayer at all, it was he—he who had not been able to protect her from the very thing that now caused these feelings. And yet, he struggled to push away the graphic pictures that imprinted themselves on his mind—unthinkable pictures of another man touching his wife in ways that made him physically shudder. And though he knew it was completely unwarranted, he felt twinges of anger at Anna, as though she should have done something herself to stop it from happening.

Of course he did not voice these unreasoned thoughts to Anna. They remained quietly below the surface of his consciousness, nagging and worrisome.

The girls went back to school on Sunday afternoon. They had stayed in Chicago for an entire week, and Anna felt guilty for causing them to miss so many days of work and school. But no amount of pleading had convinced them to leave before the weekend was over. And it *had* been nice to have their company and the distraction their presence provided.

But when they'd gone, Anna felt vulnerable and awkward with Paul. That first week, her wounds and their daughters' presence had provided excuses for avoiding romantic intimacy. But now her bruises were fading, she no longer had to wear the bandages on her neck, and she was using her arm almost normally. The question of intimacy loomed between them, a vast sea to be crossed. She and Paul had never been this reticent with each other. They always had been able to talk openly about such things.

Anna waited for Paul to approach her, to prove that he didn't see her as defiled, to prove that he didn't blame her for what had happened, that he still found her desirable.

And while she lay on her side of the bed, at once hoping and fearing that he would take her in his arms with passion rather than pity, he lay on his side, waiting for her to give him some sign that she was ready for him to touch her with love in the places where he—Anna's rapist—had touched her in violation.

They both were afraid that the precious gift of lovemaking they'd always shared had been stolen from them forever on that awful night in Orlando.

—⟶⟵—

Paul came home from work early on Friday night. Anna

heard the car pull in the driveway and went to the window. She watched him park the car in the drive, open the door, and reach across the seat for a bulky package wrapped in green tissue paper. Flowers?

She hurried to the door to meet him, curious about the bundle now tucked under his arm alongside his briefcase. Paul smiled at his wife and wordlessly held the bouquet out to her—freesia and dainty sprigs of sweet-smelling pink jasmine that were her favorite.

"Mmm, they're beautiful, Paul!" She buried her nose in the fragrant blossoms and took them from his arms with a questioning smile. "Our anniversary isn't for another three months, honey." It really wasn't like Paul to buy her flowers for no reason.

He leaned across the bouquet of flowers and kissed her, crushing the florist's wrapping between them. "Does it have to be a special occasion for a man to buy flowers for his wife?" he teased.

"Well, no, but for this man it usually is" She poked him in the chest, mimicking his playful tone.

She turned to rummage in the cupboard for a vase, but Paul was right behind her, nuzzling her neck, brushing her hair away from the nape of her neck and tracing the thin scar with his kisses, whispering in her ear. The playfulness was gone now, and Anna heard the emotion in his voice. "Anna, I love you. I love you so much. All week I've been thinking of how close I came to losing you..." He choked on the words. Her name was a low moan in his throat. "Oh, Anna... Anna ..."

Her heart soared, suddenly *knowing* that his love for her had not changed. She dropped the bouquet on the counter and turned and hugged him to her with all her strength. Pain seared through her still-tender shoulder, but the pain didn't matter now. She put her hands on the back of her husband's neck and combed her fingers through his sandy hair.

Paul held her at arm's length and looked down at her,

his green eyes intense. She saw such love, such gentleness in those eyes.

"Anna, I don't want to rush you… I don't… I don't know for sure how to *be* with you. But I *miss* you. I miss you so much."

The meaning in his words, in his caress was unmistakable, and Anna felt desire rise in her. For one sharp moment the veil of the terror in Orlando threatened to choke out that desire.

But then Paul's gentle hands were on her again, his voice low and full of love. The rough grip of the rapist, the evil touch of that *monster* had not resembled this in any way. Her attacker's hands had not caressed her, had not *loved* her this way, had not touched her gently in intimate places as her husband did now.

Oh, how grateful she was in this moment for the sweet lovemaking of her husband, for it in no way resembled the violence of the attack and the pain *he* had inflicted on her.

Paul took her hand in his own and led her—willing, longing—to their bedroom.

Anna awoke the next morning full of hope. They'd cleared a difficult hurdle so easily. And regained one precious part of their life "before." In her mind, Anna put the phrase in quotes: "Life before the attack." Strange how a traumatic event separated your life into distinct eras—before and after.

What a comfort it was now to have the gift of their tender physical union after such a brutal physical violation. She breathed a prayer of thanks and, perhaps naively, believed she'd won the battle—that it might all be over now.

Later that morning as she hung fresh laundry in their closet, she discovered the shopping bag that held her purchases from Orlando. The EMTs who'd answered the ambulance call had recovered Anna's purse and packages, untouched, from the alley behind the mall. Paul must have put the shopping bag in the back of their closet when he unpacked their suitcases.

Now Anna dragged the bag from the closet. The outside of the glossy rope-handled bag was scuffed and streaked with dirt. Someplace in her mind the reason for the marks registered. Handling the bag gingerly, and trembling unreasonably, she pulled out the items she'd purchased that day one by one.

The new sunglasses, long forgotten, were on the top inside a smaller bag, enfolded in layers of tissue paper. Without unwrapping them, she dropped them back into the larger bag. She pulled out three summer tops, gaily colored pastels in spring colors. She held each one in front of her and with unfocused eyes, she stared into the face of that awful day, remembering how her carefree shopping trip had ended.

With a ferocity the empowered her, she stuffed the shirts into the bag, crumpled the whole package into a wad, and hurried out to the garage with it. She jammed it into the large steel garbage can, hiding the wad beneath a pile of old newspapers. As she pushed it still deeper under the newspapers, she felt the lenses in the sunglasses crack beneath her clenched fist, but she gave no thought to the money she'd spent on them or on the clothes. She didn't even consider offering the tops to her sister or to one of her daughters. She wanted no part of anything that would remind her of Orlando. The very name of the city had become obscene to her.

She came into the kitchen and washed her hands under hot running water, scrubbing her skin until it was red.

That night she dreamed again of the shrouded monster who chased her down a dark alley. And she awoke wondering if this nightmare would ever truly be over.

—⁓—

Anna sat in the doctor's waiting room leafing through magazines, not really seeing anything on the pages, lost in thought. More than three weeks had passed since her ordeal, and now her own physician in Chicago, Dr. Blakeman, had called to tell her that the tests had come back from the Orlando hospital. He'd encouraged her to schedule an appointment so he could be sure she was healing properly. He was quick to assure her on the phone that all the results looked normal, and that he didn't expect to find any problems.

She knew she looked good. The wound on her neck was a faint line now, slightly pink, but promising to fade almost completely. She still favored her left arm a bit, but she could tell it was getting stronger daily. The bruises had faded into nothing, and her face was tanned from several afternoons spent outdoors readying the ground for her flower garden.

The nightmares still came occasionally, usually with no provocation she could discern, but except for that, she was beginning to feel life was almost back to normal.

The warmth and intimacy with Paul had truly been reclaimed in that one sweet evening. Now she felt they had settled comfortably into their familiar roles with each other.

If Paul treated her differently at all, it was with a new measure of protectiveness. He had always been somewhat protective of her, and the girls, too, in a healthy sort of way. Now, he didn't want her driving alone at night, didn't want her walking alone any time of the day. He called home often during the workday, ostensibly to ask about the mail, or to have her look up some trivial piece of information—a phone number or bank balance. But she wasn't fooled by his ruses. She knew that he was checking on her. And in some ways, his caution kept her from being able to put her own fears aside. And it gave her a vague sense of guilt, as though he didn't quite trust *her.*

She'd both dreaded and welcomed this appointment with Dr. Blakeman. She remembered the word *closure* from a psychology lecture. That was what she needed. A sense that this was the final step in her healing—a clean bill of health—and then she could put it all behind her forever.

A nurse poked her head through the door, caught Anna's eye, and softly mouthed her name. Dr. Blakeman had been the Marquette family's doctor since the girls were small, and his nurses knew each of them by name. Now their familiarity was comforting, and somehow, uncharacteristically, she felt no embarrassment in having them know what she'd been through.

Tossing the magazine back on the table, she gathered her purse and jacket and followed the nurse down the sterile hallway to a tiny examination room. She had been waiting only a short time when Dr. Blakeman knocked softly and walked in without waiting for a reply.

"Hi, Anna. How are you getting along?"

"I'm doing fine. I really am."

"That's good." He was a man of few words, but his voice held compassion and genuine caring. He looked over Anna's charts and then closed them and looked into her eyes as he spoke. It was not disconcerting to be regarded so, but rather it comforted her and made her feel that what she was about to hear would be the truth.

"Well, Anna, as I told you on the phone, everything looks fine with all the tests that came in from Orlando. There's no sign of any disease or infection, and I think you can pretty much breathe easy that there won't be. We will want you to come in for follow-ups on a couple of the tests, but it's certainly nothing to concern yourself with." He paused and ruffled the edges of the folder that contained her medical charts. "I hate to even bring this up because I don't want to alarm you…it's just a precaution, really, but usually in cases like this we do like to run a follow-up pregnancy test."

"But…didn't they do that test in Orlando? Didn't it come back negative?" Anna asked, concern rising in her voice.

"Well, yes, it did, but actually the pregnancy test which is part of a rape kit is for the purpose of detecting an *existing* pregnancy. Should a woman become pregnant as a result of rape, it would probably not show up in test results for at least seventy-two hours. But if you took the morning-after pill, that would eliminate the possibility."

"But I didn't. I...refused it."

"I see." Dr. Blakeman looked surprised. "Well, I want to assure you that the incidence of such an occurrence is extremely rare, but I would prefer to run another pregnancy test. Just to put your mind at ease."

Anna knew her face must have reflected her growing concern because he held up his hands palms out and told her, "This is strictly a precaution. At any rate, with your permission, we can go ahead and do that today. If it should show that implantation has occurred, we can still take care of it with medication at this point. And then we can close the files on this, so to speak."

Anna was stunned. Since declining the morning-after pill that night in the hospital, she hadn't given the possibility another thought. The doctor had told her it was rare for rape to result in pregnancy. And yet, she knew it sometimes happened. Just...not to *her*.

In all the nights she'd lain awake thinking and imagining and worrying, she'd feared diseases and infections, and loathed the precautions she and Paul had had to take to protect him until they knew for sure that she was "safe."

But the crime that had been committed against her was so far removed from the lovemaking she associated with pregnancy that it hadn't even seemed a possibility. And now they were talking again about some kind of morning-after pill. Essentially *abortion*.

What else haven't I thought of? Will this nightmare ever end?

She shook herself back to the present and managed a calm reply, hardly hearing Dr. Blakeman's words as he briefly examined her and ordered yet another blood test from the lab. He assured her again that it was only a precaution. "You can call for the results this afternoon."

—⚏—

Anna treated herself to lunch at a new deli that had opened up near the doctor's office. After picking up a few groceries, she drove home, put the food away, sorted through the mail, and then, determined to treat the call with indifference, she dialed the clinic.

"Lakeland Clinic. Which doctor, please?"

"I'm calling for lab results. I'm Dr. Blakeman's patient."

"One moment, please. I'll connect you with his nurse."

A short burst of symphony music was followed by a series of clicks.

"Dr. Blakeman's office. This is Claire."

"Hi. This is Anna Marquette. I'm just calling for results from the lab work I had done this morning."

Anna could hear the hesitation on the other end. Silence. Not Claire's usual cheery "Oh, hi, Anna. Just a minute, I'll see if I can find them," but rather a blaring silence.

"Urn…Anna, can you hold for just a minute?" Claire finally said.

"Yes, I'll hold." She willed herself to stay calm, to not jump to any hasty conclusions, but her hands were shaking. Moments later, Dr. Blakeman's soothing voice came on the line.

"Anna? Hi. Listen, I hate to have to do this, but it appears there's been some kind of problem with the lab work. I'd like you to come in so we can repeat a test we ran this morning. I do apologize for putting you through this. I know you were hoping to be done with this today. If you could possibly come back in within the next hour or so, we might be able to have the results yet this evening. Otherwise, come at your convenience tomorrow. Either way, you can just go straight to the lab. Since it's a repeat I won't need to see you again."

Anna felt reassured by his calmness, his apologies. It was just a mix-up. It happened all the time in medical labs. Didn't it? There was nothing to worry about. But she did want to be done with it today. She didn't want to spend a sleepless night worrying.

"I'll come right away, if that's okay. I don't have any other plans, so it's no problem."

"That would be fine. We'll do our best to let you know yet today. Again, I do apologize for the inconvenience."

She drove to the clinic, completed the test again, and was back home preparing supper when Paul pulled into the driveway at six. He knew that she'd had an appointment with Dr. Blakeman that morning and casually asked her how it had gone.

"Everything went fine. All the tests from Orlando came back okay, and he basically gave me a clean bill of health."

He gave her a hug. "Oh, that's great, honey. I'm so glad that's over with. Are you doing okay?" He held her away from himself and looked into her eyes.

She opened her mouth to tell him about the unexpected pregnancy test, but he looked so hopeful and things felt so close between them that she hated to ruin the mood. Instead, she gave him a smile and drew his arms back around her, snuggling into his warmth.

They were in the middle of supper when the phone rang. Anna had almost put the test out of her mind, but before she picked up the phone, she remembered and knew that this would be the lab.

"Anna?"

It was Dr. Blakeman's voice. An alarm went off somewhere inside her head.

"Yes. This is Anna."

"Anna. I'm afraid I have some bad news for you. Is someone there with you?"

"Yes. Paul's here..." Her mouth went dry and cottony, and her words trailed off weakly.

"Anna, the pregnancy test came back positive. The first one we did this morning turned out positive, and I thought it must be a mix-up. But now the new test is reading positive as well. There's always a chance it could still be a mistake, but I'd like to see you in my office just to confirm this one way or another."

"But…what…what are you saying? Are you saying I'm… pregnant?"

"Well, like I said, I'd like to see you so we can be sure. But yes… That's what the tests are indicating."

The room spun. She held the phone out and croaked Paul's name.

He rushed to her side and took the receiver from her hand. She slumped into a kitchen chair as the buzzing in her head drowned out Paul's murmured conversation with Dr. Blakeman.

Eight

On Thursday morning, for the second time in as many days, Anna sat in Dr. Blakeman's waiting room. This time Paul was at her side. Neither of them had slept last night, and yet in all the hours of tossing and turning and pacing the floor, they had not been able to talk about the shadow looming over them.

Paul was taking the attitude that they would deal with it when they knew for certain that it was a fact. Anna was too shaken to have any attitude at all. She now knew the meaning of the old cliche: it was all like a bad dream. Only she hadn't slept, so there would be no awakening from this nightmare.

After an interminable wait, they were ushered into an examination room. The nurse handed Anna a flimsy hospital gown and asked Paul to wait outside.

Dr. Blakeman examined her in silence while a nurse stood at her side, offering to hold her hand. Anna was too numb to voice any of the questions that catapulted through her mind. She barely remembered getting dressed and being led with Paul to the doctor's private office, but now they sat in front of his desk in large upholstered chairs, fingers entwined, exchanging pained glances. But they sat in silence.

Ten minutes later, Dr. Blakeman opened the door and made his way to the swivel chair behind his desk. He settled into his chair with the labored breathing and heavy sigh of a harried and troubled man. He looked at the open folder in front of him as though it were a script that would give him the words to say.

"I'm afraid it doesn't look good," he said finally. "It's very early to be seeing any obvious symptoms of a pregnancy, but my examination does confirm what the tests are telling us. And since Paul had the vasectomy, let's see"—he leafed through the folder—"seven years ago, almost eight, I think you know what that means. There are tests we could do to verify paternity, but they're expensive, and they take sometimes weeks to get results. I assume you'd like to take care of this as soon as possible, and from a medical point of view, that would, of course, be in your best interest, Anna."

He rested his elbows on the desk in front of him, hands clasped, his index fingers forming a steeple. He studied them for a minute, and when he spoke again, his voice was so quiet Anna had to strain to hear his words. "I'll be honest with you. In twenty-two years of practicing medicine, this is the first time I have ever been faced with a situation like this. I don't know what your views are on abortion. Ordinarily, I'm opposed to it, but if ever there were a case where it would be justified—"

Why was he talking about abortion? Anna couldn't seem to catch her breath. She squeezed Paul's hand and tried to make sense of what the doctor was saying.

Dr. Blakeman cleared his throat. "Unfortunately, we're too close to the cutoff for me to feel completely comfortable with the abortion pill option… While I don't perform abortions myself, I can refer you to someone right here in the clinic who does. This early on, it would be a fairly simple procedure—done on an outpatient basis. You would be back home in a few hours. Within a week, ten days, you should feel pretty much back to normal. It may take your menstrual cycle a while to regulate itself, but you should feel up to doing just about anything you usually do within a week or so."

Dr. Blakeman paused and looked directly at Anna. "If you should decide to abort the pregnancy, I would want to do a careful medical history on you, Anna—especially if there is any history of breast cancer in your family. You may be aware that studies have shown a possible link between abortion and breast cancer. It's a controversial topic, and of course there's some risk involved in carrying a pregnancy to term at your age, but we would need to weigh those risks, and I think it only fair that you be made aware of the risks with both factors."

In stunned silence, Anna listened to the verdict, listened to the offered solution. It didn't seem possible this could be happening to them. This was the stuff magazine articles were made of. This was a hypothetical question in one of Anna's situational ethics classes. It didn't happen to real people. Certainly not to them.

Paul had let go of her hand when Dr. Blakeman came into the room. Now he reached for it again. He cleared his throat. "This is too much for us to deal with right now. We… we're going to have to go home and talk this over…think it through before we make any decisions." He stood and pulled Anna up beside him. Then turning back to the doctor in a last plea for hope, he asked, "You're sure there could be no mistake about this?"

"You mean about the existence of a pregnancy?"

Paul nodded.

"No, there's no mistake. We can run the test one more time if you want us to. I understand your wanting to be absolutely certain. But the test is rarely falsely positive. The due date would be December 13."

Anna sat stunned. Hearing that date—a due date—made

it all too real. By Christmas—if they didn't do something—they would have a baby. *She* would have a baby.

"I know it must seem unbelievable to both of you at this point," the doctor said. "I'm sorry, but…" He shrugged, apparently at a loss for any words that would offer them any comfort.

Paul rose and offered his outstretched hand, but Anna could tell it was taking everything he had to compose himself. "Thank you," he said. "We…we'll let you know what we decide."

Dr. Blakeman opened the door for them, and they walked down the long corridor to the outer waiting room, Paul's arm protectively around her. She bent her head to hide the tears.

They drove the short distance home in silence. But when they pulled into their driveway, she crumbled. "What are we going to do, Paul? I don't understand why this is happening. Haven't we been through enough already? Why us? How could God do this to us?" Her voice climbed a pitch with each question.

Paul put the car in park, reaching for her across the console. "I don't know, babe. I don't know… All I know is that I would do *anything* to have spared you this whole ordeal. I don't know what we're going to do, but we'll get through this somehow…somehow *together*, with God's help, we'll get through it. I promise you that." He held her head against his chest and stroked her hair away from her face.

Anna felt stronger in his arms, but— If Paul didn't know how they would get through it, any hope she'd had earlier dissipated like morning mist.

—⁂—

They went through the motions that night—fixing sandwiches for supper, cleaning up the kitchen together, watching the news, getting ready for bed. They ate little, spoke little, and touched often, taking comfort in each other's very presence. There seemed to be an unspoken agreement between them that the time for talking would make itself known, and until then they would hang on to a thread of hope so thin it didn't seem capable of holding one of them, let alone both.

After she'd washed her face and brushed her teeth, Anna walked through the rooms of their house in her nightgown and robe. Everything was so sweetly familiar to her tonight—the round oak table that had belonged to her grandparents. The pillows on the sofa, painstakingly embroidered in shades of pink and deep rose by Paul's mother. The clock—a wedding gift—sounding its comforting cadence on the mantel. This little house on Fairmont Avenue in their quiet Chicago neighborhood had always been a haven from the storms of life. Even after they'd come home from Orlando and the horror that had happened there, after that first week of fearfulness, she had felt enveloped once again by the safety of this home and the people who came and went from here.

Was there finally an intruder so evil, so horrible that it could penetrate not only this house, but her very body?

Shivering, she walked through the house and checked all the locks, turned out the lights, then went back to their bedroom. Paul was already in bed, propped on pillows against the headboard. He turned down the blankets on her side of the bed and patted the place where she usually lay.

"Come here."

She turned off the lights, leaving the room in the dim glow of Paul's reading lamp. She crawled into bed, found the cradle of her husband's shoulder, and there the words began to flow—a trickle at first, building word on thought on emotion. But then they came in a rush, like the breaking of a dam.

"Are you okay?" How many hundred times had he asked her that question in the past weeks?

She shook her head against his chest. "It's not real to me yet, Paul. I think I'm in shock. I don't... I don't *feel* pregnant."

"Have you thought at all about what Dr. Blakeman was suggesting?"

"You mean…abortion?" She could barely bring herself to whisper the word.

"I'd want to do some research before I looked at it that way." He rubbed his temples.

"It's strange…" She bit her lip. "It's always seemed like… such a horrible thing. I mean we've talked about it so many times—in church, with the girls—how wrong it is. It's always seemed like such a drastic decision. But… I don't know…"

"I'll be honest, babe. I can't imagine any other option at this point. I just keep thinking that this could all be over…we could go forward from here."

She nodded. "I know. I don't know if I'm strong enough to face anything else. But…we've always said we were against it. We've preached to the girls about how immoral it is…the easy way out and all that. Maybe if I *felt* pregnant I wouldn't be saying this, but …" She hesitated. What she was about to say seemed heretical. "Is there anything there yet, Paul? I mean, is it really… a *baby* this early?"

"He's probably right, honey. If we take care of it right away, it's easier all the way around."

Anna started crying then. "Paul, listen to us. Have we been wrong in our view of abortion all these years? Have we been judgmental all along? Are we seeing a new side to this that's really changing our minds? Or are we just justifying what would be the easy way out of this? I'm so confused." She buried her face in her hands.

"Okay."

Paul's voice took on a no-nonsense tenor. He was an executive in control of a meeting now. And she needed his clear, analytical thinking.

"Let's at least lay all the options on the table," he said. "We—you could have the abortion, and it'll all be over and done with, and this time next month our lives will be relatively back to normal. No one would need to know. That's one option."

"Or we can carry this through," he continued. "Maybe

you will miscarry, Anna. That surely could happen with all the stress you've been under. Maybe we should *pray* for that."

"Paul, that just sounds awful to pray for something like that!"

"I know. I know." He held his palms toward her in a posture of apology. "I'm sorry, Anna, but I...Anna, I just can't picture a baby at the end of all this. I'm sorry. I just cannot." His voice had risen, but now it was a whisper. "Especially not another man's baby...especially not that."

"Oh, Paul. I can't blame you for that. I *don't* blame you."

"And what if there's something genetic that caused that man to...attack you? Could we be bringing something even more evil into the world?"

She hadn't thought of that. Was there such a thing as a "bad seed"? She didn't know.

They lay together in silence, utterly exhausted. They hadn't slept more than a few hours at a time since Orlando. And now they seemed to be going around in circles. Every thought they gave voice to brought them back to where they'd started.

Paul reached up and switched off his reading lamp. "Anna, we can't make a decision like this overnight. And right now we're trying to think clearly on virtually no sleep. We can't rush into anything, and neither of us is in any shape to think straight right now, let alone make a decision of this magnitude. We'll do the right thing. That's all I can promise you. We'll do the right thing," he said again, as if saying it might guarantee its truth.

"Paul, please pray for me. I've...I've tried to pray since we left the doctor's office, but I can't seem to. It's not that I'm mad at God. At least I don't think I blame Him for any of this. But I just can't pray. I know I need to, but I can't. I... I don't know where God is in all this... It almost seems like this is too...*ugly* for Him to hear."

The tears came again. And as she wept, she could feel Paul's chest heave in grief beneath her. Her hot tears fell on

his bare skin, but he held her tightly to him, and she somehow knew that he was praying as he had never prayed before.

Nine

They slept fitfully until Paul's alarm jangled them awake at seven. It was Friday, and Paul offered to stay home from work, but Anna couldn't ask that of him when he'd missed so many days of work already, staying home while she was recovering from Orlando, then accompanying her to the doctor yesterday. He couldn't very well offer an honest explanation to the agency either. He'd given them a vague excuse, using Anna's doctor's appointments as his reason.

She knew he was behind on some important projects at work, and besides, they had the weekend ahead of them. Besides, she needed some time alone to sort things out. She hushed his protests and kissed him goodbye as cheerfully as she could manage.

She stacked the breakfast dishes in the dishwasher and poured herself a second cup of coffee. She carried it into the living room and sat down on the sofa. The sunlight was so beautiful this time of morning, filtering through the layers of lace at the front windows. She'd always loved this room, filled with wonderful reminders of her family. She had known such happiness in her life. Was it all about to end? To crumble around her?

Her thoughts turned back to her conversation with Paul the night before. If only she could talk to someone else. Someone who wasn't emotionally involved in their situation. But if they decided to go through with the abortion, she knew they would never tell anyone. They would never speak of it again. And that was part of the horror of even considering such a solution.

Oh, how she hated secrets. All her life, even happy secrets—like surprise birthday parties or Christmas gifts—had made her feel on edge, afraid she would slip and reveal too much. She hated feeling she had to carefully measure every word she spoke. Yet this was certainly not the kind of thing you told. Even their own daughters must not know if they decided to go through with it. How hypocritical would this be, after all their moralizing and lectures.

But there *were* no other choices! She was forty-five years old. Even if she could go through the pregnancy at her age, this child would not belong to Paul. She didn't blame him for not wanting to even think of her bearing a child like that. Who knew what kind of person it might turn out to be? She'd searched the internet this morning, typing in the phrase: *Is criminal behavior hereditary?* What she'd found left her more frightened and confused than ever.

What about adoption? That was something they hadn't talked about yet. But they'd have to reveal the truth about the baby's…*heritage*. Wouldn't they? Would anyone want the child of a rapist? Were such babies adoptable? But even if they were, she couldn't go through a pregnancy here. She would have to go into exile. She simply could not face her friends, her classmates at the university, people at their church, her parents… *Oh, dear God, her parents!*

They'd decided not to tell Anna's parents about the rape. Jack and Charlotte Greyson lived two hours from Chicago.

They were retired but healthy and active. Her parents were dear to her, but her mother was such a worrier, and she had her hands full caring for her own mother who was ninety-six and in frail health. Anna hadn't felt anything would be gained by telling them.

They'd told very few people of the attack. The girls, of course, and Paul's mother. Anna was very close to her mother-in-law, seeing her as a friend more than a mother figure. Even so, they hadn't even intended to tell even her. But Shirley Marquette had stopped by for an unexpected visit a few days after the attack, and of course there had to be an explanation for Anna's bruises and bandages. In the end, they'd told her everything, and Anna was glad her mother-in-law knew. Shirley had been unwavering in her support at a time when Anna needed that strength desperately. But Shirley would never understand the unspeakable thing they were actually considering now. *No.* If they did this thing, no one could ever know. *No one.*

And it was that thought that led Anna to realize that she simply could not do it. If abortion was so unutterable that they could tell no one, how could she live with a secret like that for the rest of her life? And of course, God would know.

Anna set her coffee cup on the floor and stretched out on the sofa, exhausted from the weight of the decision. The morning light intensified and fell across her stockinged feet. Silvery dust particles danced in the brightness. Finally, in a state that wasn't quite sleep but wasn't really waking either, Anna dreamed, or rather, she remembered. Long ago, and hidden far in the secret recesses of her mind, lay a fragile memory. Now it pushed its way into her consciousness.

Many years ago when she and Paul were newly married, Anna had a miscarriage. They had not planned for her to get pregnant. Yet when it happened, they were excited. They would make the best of things. They would welcome this unexpected baby.

And as the days went by, she began to feel there was nothing she could imagine loving more than having Paul's baby and being a mother. But when she was in her third month, before they'd even told anyone she was pregnant, Anna had begun to bleed. Lightly at first. Nothing to be alarmed about, the doctor said. But then in the middle of the night, a sudden, excruciating pain gripped her. She felt the contractions of birth, unknown to her before this night. And somehow she knew with certainty that she was losing their baby. Paul had held her and tried to comfort her. She was deeply disappointed, already feeling a bond with the little life that grew inside her, already excitedly making plans for this surprise in their lives.

It had been horrifying to realize that her body was expelling her dream, and she was helpless to stop it. Yet there was astonishment and wonder at the tiny, perfectly formed baby that had come forth from her body that night. Tiny fingers and toes outlined beneath the diaphanous sac that encased it. She hadn't known it would be like this. It was disturbing, and yet she was awestruck. *This was a child.* In all the weeks of daydreaming about their child-to-be, it had never quite seemed real to her that she was carrying a baby. And now, here was the reality lying on their bed. Paul had seen it too. Trembling, she'd wrapped the tiny form in a cloth and taken it with them to the hospital, as her doctor had instructed. Afterward, she'd wanted so desperately to ask what had been done with the baby's body. But she didn't ask.

And she and Paul had never spoken of it again. Oh, they'd talked about the miscarriage. And had told their daughters, when they were older, about the earlier lost pregnancy. But never again had she and Paul spoken to each other, or to anyone else, about that translucent, flawless, tiny body.

Anna sat up on the sofa with a start, fully awake now. *No!* She could not allow this little intruder to be flushed from her body—no matter how unwelcome he or she might be. With her miscarriage she'd not had a say in the decision. And now that the choice was in her hands to make, she knew she could not play God. It was not this baby's fault it had been conceived.

Anna thought of her own two daughters. What precious blessings they were. How tiny and perfect they'd been when they were placed in her arms moments after birth. The child she carried now was no less her own than Kara and Kassandra were. This dawning knowledge washed over her, and an icy finger of chill raced down her spine.

No. No. She could not allow her own flesh and blood to be destroyed, no matter the details of the conception. She suddenly knew that with more certainty than she'd ever known anything in her life.

So now she had to think about what it would mean to go through with the pregnancy. It was almost laughable. Her friends were beginning to welcome grandchildren! And maternity clothes? It seemed silly to envision herself ballooning, waddling, wearing the wardrobe of a young mother-to-be. She thought of Kara's married friend who'd worn such form-fitting tops during her pregnancy that the outline of her navel was clear to all. Anna actually felt her face grow warm at the thought. Even if she wore more conservative clothing, it would be humiliating. Paul would be embarrassed.

Anna went through the day in turmoil, wavering between disbelief and acceptance, one decision and then another. But with the realization that she could not bring herself to end this pregnancy came a tentative, fragile peace.

Paul arrived home early, and Anna could tell, watching him walk into the house, that he'd thought of little else all day. The hunch of his broad shoulders and the dark circles under his eyes testified what his casual greeting tried to deny.

"Hi, babe." He gave her his usual greeting kiss and a sad smile. "How are you doing? Do you have this figured out yet?"

"I have some thoughts. But I want to hear what you've been thinking first."

Paul put his briefcase on the floor and shrugged off his

jacket and hung it on the hook by the door. He slumped onto a stool at the kitchen counter. "Oh, Anna. I don't know what to think. I have to admit that I've given a lot of thought—a lot—to ending the pregnancy. I think it might be acceptable in this case. I mean…it's not the perfect solution. I know it won't be as easy as that. I wish there was some other way, but I can't see it, Anna."

He rubbed his temples. "I wonder just how risky it would be for you to go through a pregnancy at your age?" Anger crept into his voice. "I won't lose you over this, Anna. I won't!"

"You're not going to lose me." She felt stronger just speaking the words.

He sighed and put his head in his hands. "There are just too many things to face if we choose any other route. Every time I think about you going through with it, I hit a brick wall. I can't see it." He searched her eyes. "Don't you feel that way, Anna? I don't see that we *have* a choice. Don't you agree that ending the pregnancy is really the only way we *can* go?"

"No, Paul." The strength in her tone surprised her. And Paul too, judging by the way he looked at her. "I cannot have an abortion," she said.

"You sound…so certain. Have you really thought this through? What kind of future would the baby have? What would we tell people? What would we tell the girls? They know about my vasectomy. They would know the baby couldn't be mine."

"I think we'd have to be honest."

As if he hadn't heard her, he went on. "I don't know if this child would have a chance in the world of turning out okay. Its father is a rapist… a criminal! People would eventually find out. And how could you ever explain that—to the kid?" His face was flushed, and his voice trembled in a way that frightened her.

She moved toward him, but he held his arms rigid in front of him.

She shrank back as the words tumbled from his lips in

a flood, as though he might lose his opportunity to speak them if he didn't do so quickly. "I don't know if evil traits are hereditary or not, but, Anna, I'm afraid no one would want to adopt a child conceived in rape. And I'm not sure I could love it. I don't think I could pretend. That's asking too much, Anna…too much …" He let out a frayed breath and hung his head, exhausted and obviously overcome with emotion.

A flash of insight penetrated Anna's mind. She went to him, put a hand on his shoulder, testing his receptiveness to her touch. When he didn't spurn her, she took his face in her hands and spoke quietly, making her voice firm. "Paul, you don't think a child born of a horrible, abusive criminal, a child raised by a man who is not his real father has any hope for the future? Go look in the mirror, honey! This is *your* story!"

It was true. Paul's father had brutally beaten his mother—literally within an inch of her life—when she was pregnant with Paul. When she'd been released from the hospital after nearly losing the baby, Shirley had fled to the safety of her parents' home. There, when Paul was just a few months old, she met Albert Marquette. They fell in love, were married as soon as Shirley's divorce became final, and on Paul's first birthday, Albert legally adopted him, proudly giving him the Marquette name. Paul had never known anything but uncon-ditional love from his adoptive father. Albert, fifteen years Shirley's senior, died when Paul was in college, but there was no denying that he was far more a father to Paul than the man whose genes Paul carried. And Paul had the gentle spirit and compassionate ways of the father with whom he shared not a drop of blood.

Paul looked at her, obviously as stunned as she'd been by the revelation. "But it wasn't all a bed of roses. I went through a hard time of searching. A kid can't help but wonder about his biological father."

Anna knew that was true. Shirley had told Paul his histo-ry when he was a young teenager. And though he knew she'd

told the truth about his birth father, sometimes—especially when he was at odds with Albert—he pretended that his
"real" father had been falsely accused or misunderstood. But
as he grew to manhood, he knew in his heart that the ugly
story was true. He'd come to accept his heritage and to realize
that his true legacy had been conferred by Albert Marquette.
And he'd loved the man for it.

"There's something else, Paul." Trembling, Anna recounted her remembrance of the miscarriage from earlier that day.
"I… I hadn't thought about it for so many years, and you and
I… we never really did talk about it. But don't you remember, Paul? Don't you remember seeing it on our bed after I
miscarried? *That was a baby*, Paul! It wasn't a blob of tissue.
It was a perfectly formed baby. I held that tiny body in my
hands. That's what we would be destroying if I had an abortion." Her voice broke, and she fell silent, incredulous all over
again at the memory.

—⁂—

Paul stared at Anna, bewildered. He hadn't thought about
her miscarriage for many years, but with her quiet words, the
images came vividly to his mind. He ignored the stab of guilt
that came with the memory.

But *that* baby had been wanted, excitedly looked forward to. This was surely different. Yet Anna sounded so convinced—no, *convicted* was the word. It truly frightened him
to hear the certainty in her voice. In all the wild, disconnected thoughts that had swirled through his head since they'd
learned the news of Anna's pregnancy, it had never occurred
to him that he might not have any say in their decision. Of
course, he would never force his wife to have an abortion
against her will. And yet this situation intimately involved
him. Affected his life as deeply as it affected hers.

He sighed. "I understand why you might feel this way.
Honestly, I do. But I'm afraid your emotions are clouding

your judgment."

She stared at him, as though she couldn't believe what she was hearing. Tears welled in her eyes. "You can't mean that."

"Anna, *think* about it." Now he was angry. Couldn't she see that this was an impossible situation? Surely she couldn't be serious about carrying this pregnancy to term. It was ludicrous! In fact, it was purely selfish for her to consider such a thing.

"I *have* thought about it, Paul. I have." Her tone was even, but he heard the hurt in her voice.

He could see they were getting nowhere with this discussion. It would do him no good to argue with her now. She'd let her feelings carry her wisdom away, and he knew his wife well enough to understand that she could not be reasoned with when she was in a highly emotional state.

He slid off the kitchen stool and pulled his jacket from the hook. "We'll talk about it later," he said. "This conversation is not getting us anywhere."

He left her standing at the counter, openmouthed and in tears. The screen door slammed behind him, and he took off at a jog down the driveway. He didn't look back but ran, faster and faster, trying to outdistance the piercing guilt that dogged him.

Because of the Rain

Ten

Paul ran to the end of their street and stopped, out of breath. He felt guilty for walking out on Anna in the middle of an argument. He knew she hated that reaction even more than seeing his anger flare. It was something that came up again and again when they talked about their relationship. Running away had always been his first resort to avoid dealing with issues.

But sometimes Anna simply would not listen to reason. Sometimes his leaving cleared the air for both of them, and often, when he came back to her, whatever they had been fighting about seemed silly and juvenile.

An overpowering weariness came over him as he realized that whatever the ultimate outcome, this argument, in retrospect, would never seem petty or juvenile. Their decision—regardless of who won the argument this time—would change their lives forever, one way or another. They were talking literally about life and death.

There. He'd said it. Despite the remarks he had made with

such zeal to Anna, in the back of his mind, he knew that even if abortion might be justified in this case, it was still a death sentence for one. He and Anna might be able to eventually get over the trauma of the whole ordeal of the rape, even the trauma of a decision to abort. But unless they could lie convincingly to themselves, Paul knew they would have to accept the truth: if they chose to abort, a human life *would* be taken as atonement for one evil man's sin. Would that innocent life be on Paul's head forever? And even if God did forgive him, would his conscience ever allow him to put the guilt of the deed behind him? He wasn't sure.

Though Anna truly was his first consideration, in many ways he was being selfish. He had tried to lay the label of selfishness on her, but he knew his accusation was grossly misplaced. He was the one who was fleeing from the inconvenience and the trauma of this situation.

He'd been honest when he told Anna that he could not imagine a baby—another child—at the end of this hazy, uncertain journey. He didn't *want* to imagine that. It would be *beyond* imagining to have Anna go through such a pregnancy in front of their friends, in their neighborhood, in their church. He couldn't begin to envision how they could explain their situation to their closest friends, let alone curious acquaintances or his associates at Lindell & Bachman.

But he wasn't thinking *only* of himself. He truly was concerned about the future of a child born into such circumstances. This would have been hard enough if it was *his* child. But there was Anna's health to consider. He didn't know all the medical ramifications of pregnancy at forty-five, but he'd read enough to know that it held at least some physical risks, apart from the social and emotional ones.

He turned and jogged back toward home, his head swimming with conflicting thoughts. He felt powerless to sort them out, to make any sense of them whatsoever. He couldn't remember feeling such turmoil since the night he'd discovered the truth about his birth father. Finally, he trudged back up the driveway and lowered himself wearily onto the concrete steps of the back porch.

He put his head in his hands, unable to physically hold it up any longer. "God, I can't deal with this! Please don't ask me to go through this. Help me, Lord…help me…help us …" His spirit pled eloquently with the Almighty, but the sounds that came from his lips were unintelligible moans of anguish.

He wasn't sure how long he sat that way, but the sky was already darkening when he became aware of Anna's hands on his shoulders. Up and down Fairmont Avenue, streetlights had begun to flicker on, casting patchy shadows over the rows of greening lawns.

"Paul?" Her voice quivered with recently shed tears. Again, he felt guilt gouge him with an almost physical pain. What was wrong with him? She needed him, and he'd run away from home like a petulant child.

Wordless, he pulled her down beside him on the steps, hugging her close. They sat in silence, listening to the sounds of their neighborhood: lawn sprinklers chirring through their cycles, distant traffic, the occasional high-pitched barking of a dog.

Finally he broke the silence. "I'm sorry I ran out on you again, babe." He squeezed her shoulder and was grateful to read forgiveness in her response. She put her arm tightly around his waist and rested her head on his shoulder.

"I'm ashamed," he continued. "It's pretty sad that I'm having a more difficult time dealing with this than you are. I'm jealous of your conviction. I wish I felt so certain that everything would turn out for good. I can't say that. Not with conviction. On an intellectual level, I know that God has never let us down yet. I do believe His promise that all things work together for good, but… This is going to require a step of faith I'm not sure I'm capable of taking."

Anna pulled back to look at him and smiled sadly. "That's just it, honey. There isn't a step to take. Doing the right thing now simply means we don't do anything." She patted her stomach. "This baby *will* grow and...be born. Unless we stop it."

Strangely, he felt the smallest seed of peace plant itself firmly in his heart. Anna was right. The course was already set. This life had already begun. Unless they made a conscious decision to end its life, this child was already a reality.

A thought came to him: God, in His great power, could have reached out His hand and prevented Anna's rape, and likewise, He could have prevented the resulting pregnancy. Paul didn't pretend to fathom a loving God's reasons for allowing such a tragedy, but because it had been allowed to touch their lives, surely God must have an answer and a purpose in it all. A tiny spark of faith flared within him, assuring him that what he had always believed remained true: his life and Anna's were ultimately in God's hands—a place of utmost security. He didn't know yet what the answers to their dilemma were, but he knew they were there to be discovered.

In that moment, a process began. And little by little, as an act of his will, Paul relinquished a small part of his stubborn self-sufficiency and gave it over to his God.

After many minutes, he put his arm around the woman he loved more than his own life. He pulled her head to his shoulder. "I love you, Anna. Please be patient with me."

—m—

The blare of Paul's alarm woke Anna. She heard him grumbling around the room and gathering clothes from his drawers, then the drone of the shower lulled her back to sleep. The next thing she remembered was his quick goodbye kiss. He was facing a tight deadline and needed to be in the office by six. She burrowed back under the covers without bothering to reset the alarm.

At seven-thirty, she woke again with a start. She would barely have time to take a quick shower, throw on jeans and a sweater, and make a piece of toast to eat on the way to her eight-thirty class.

Despite the upheaval in their lives, the world seemed to keep right on revolving. Clients waited impatiently in Paul's office. Classes resumed at the university.

Anna had considered not going back to school after spring break since she had already missed almost a month of classes. But Paul convinced her that she needed the distraction now more than ever. And she was grateful to have the daytime hours filled with classes and lectures, and the evenings busy with catching up on homework. Today began the fifth week of classes since spring break.

Her stomach churned as the smell of toasting bread filled the kitchen. Whether it was the beginnings of morning sickness or just her nerves, she wasn't sure. She still didn't *feel* pregnant and she struggled with hoping maybe it was all just a big mistake. Grabbing her books and her purse, Anna wrapped the toast in a paper napkin, locked up the house, and hurried to the car.

She eased into the rush-hour traffic, glad that she had only a few miles to go. She found a place to park close to the building and hurried up the steps, the low heels of her leather flats echoing on the tile floor of the wide hallway. Approaching the first set of double doors to the lecture hall, she could hear that the instructor had already begun speaking. She ducked in and found an empty seat near the back of the auditorium, grateful that her first class was large—more than three hundred students—and she could slip in unnoticed.

She took out her notebook and dug in her purse for a pen. The light was dim above the seats, but in the semi-darkness Anna's eyes were drawn to a young woman sitting in the row directly in front of her. Her long dark hair fell in a silky curtain and hid her face as she furiously scribbled notes.

But what held Anna's attention was the bundle resting on her lap, strapped snugly to her chest by a sling-like harness across one shoulder. She didn't even know the right terms for current baby paraphernalia.

Anna could just see the tiny bald head peeking out of the opening at the top of the carrier. The infant was apparently sound asleep, oblivious to his surroundings. His mother looked so young! A mere girl. Anna watched them both with fascination, the professor's voice now a meaningless drone in the background.

This could be her in a few short months! The thought was surreal. Nor did it fit with the image of herself that she'd grown comfortable with—that of a reasonably attractive but definitely middle-aged woman. She had loved being a mother when the girls were small, but she had put that young maternal image aside long ago. Now she was the wife of a successful executive, a diligent student, and yes, still a mother…but to grown daughters—daughters whom she saw now more as friends than as children who needed her constant attentiveness.

She had no difficulty picturing herself with her own successful career in counseling. Though that was in the future, it seemed achievable, fitting, already a part of who she was. But with a tiny infant strapped across her bosom? She couldn't imagine returning again to that time in her life.

She remembered when she was pregnant with her daughters that the whole world had seemed pregnant. Never before had there been so many strollers in the mall, so many billowing maternity dresses walking down Chicago's windswept streets. Now that phenomenon seemed to have reared its head again. Only instead of the serene joy she'd once felt at sharing this experience with perfect strangers, she now felt alone and desolate. Where before she'd assumed that every pregnancy was as happy and wanted as hers, now she wondered at her naiveté, and supposed that each one had as mournful a story as hers behind it.

The squeaking of the folding seats and the low voices of students leaving the auditorium shook Anna from her reverie. Feeling muddled, she picked up her books and walked across campus to her next class.

Abnormal Psychology was one of Anna's favorite courses, not because of the subject matter, but because of the professor. Emma Green fascinated Anna. The woman had a lively, unassuming manner that belied her keen intelligence and wisdom. She was also one of the most beautiful women Anna had ever known. Her skin was the color of strong coffee with cream, smooth and free of wrinkles despite the fact that she was the mother of three grown children. Her ready smile revealed teeth white as milk, and her close-cropped hair sprang from her head in wayward black ringlets that formed a seemly frame for her full features.

Emma and Anna had become cautious friends over the course of two semesters. Cautious because of the precarious teacher-student boundaries that society set. But more than either wanted to admit, cautious too, because of the lines that race and economics and marital status drew for them: Anna, married with children most of her adult life. Emma, a single mother of three for even longer. Anna's comfortable financial status. Emma's struggle to make a better life for her children than she had known herself, having grown up in the squalor of the Chicago Housing Authority's tenements. Even their physical appearances were a study in contrasts: Emma's dark African American complexion and sturdy five-foot-eleven build, contrasted with Anna's fair, blue-eyed fragility.

Anna sat through the class, concentrating with some effort on the day's lecture. The class ended, and the students began to file out the door, some of them stopping to turn in papers or ask questions of Professor Green. Emma was engaged in a discussion with a young man when Anna started out the door. But as she passed by, Emma reached out and, without missing a beat in her conversation, touched Anna on the shoulder and gave her a look that said, "wait here for just a minute, please."

Anna hung back and sat down at a desk in the front row. Surreptitiously she watched her friend and teacher. Emma used her hands broadly, slender manicured fingers painting the air as she articulated her point to the student. He backed out of the room, laughing at Emma's parting joke, undisguisedly admiring his teacher.

Emma turned, still smiling, to face Anna. "Anna ..." The affectionately spoken name lingered in the space between them. Anna felt oddly like a child sent to the principal's office for a reprimand. There was questioning in Emma's eyes now. Anna smiled weakly in response, but did not speak. She didn't know what to say. She felt naked, exposed.

Abruptly, Emma sat down in the desk beside Anna. Then with uncharacteristic intimacy, she covered Anna's pale hand with her own. "I don't mean to pry, but, girl, *somethin'* is not right with you."

Rarely did Anna detect even a trace of the tenements in Emma's voice, but it was there now. And somehow it seemed endearing and familiar to her. She sighed leadenly and opened her mouth to answer, but what escaped her lips was more a sob than it was words. "Oh, Emma ..." They'd been on a first-name basis since the time Anna had remained after class for help with a paper, and they'd discovered the warm rapport between them. Now it was a comfort to utter Emma's name, and somehow the barriers that had loomed invisible between them fell away. This was a dear friend she was confiding in. "Emma, I don't know where to start. I'm...I'm pregnant!"

"Ohhh ..." The information sank in slowly and registered with a raised eyebrow and a slow, deliberate nod. "I guess that kind of puts a crimp in your career plans, huh?"

"That's not all." It seemed too terrible to put into words. "It's not just that. It...it's not Paul's baby."

The expression on Emma's face said she was assuming something very different. Anna quickly explained. "Oh no. It's not like that. I...I was raped, Emma. And now I'm pregnant."

"Oh, dear God." There was genuine compassion in the outcry. "Oh, girl... I'm so sorry." She tightened her clasp on

Anna's hands. The gesture spoke a thousand healing words.

Anna crumbled. "Paul isn't taking it very well. I've decided to carry the pregnancy to term and he's struggling with my decision. But I just can't. And now I... I don't know what's going to happen to us."

Sitting in the cold, sterile classroom, Anna poured out the story, and there was a purging of her soul in entrusting the sordid details with someone caring and sympathetic. Anna's story unfolded, with Emma interjecting sympathetic little groans and clicks of her tongue. And when Anna finished, the black woman spoke in a quiet, faraway voice.

"Anna, I know that everything you are studying about being a counselor will tell you that the worst thing you can say to someone at a time like this is 'I know how you feel,' but..." Shaking her head, Emma looked Anna in the eye and, with a sigh, breathed the phrase. "I know how you feel."

Anna shot her a questioning look.

"I was raped, too, when I was fourteen. I didn't get pregnant... at least not then, but I felt so... so dirty, so sinful, that I kind of went crazy." Emma paused, as though collecting her thoughts. But when she continued, there was quiet resolve in her voice. " You see, it was...my boyfriend who raped me. I felt so guilty that I had let him take my virginity from me. Unlike you, I *was* partly at fault. I was young and naive, and I didn't realize I was leading him on. I know now that doesn't excuse what he did, but still, the guilt was overwhelming. He was older—almost twenty. After that, I figured I was already ruined—damaged goods and all that—so I became promiscuous. And within a year I was pregnant with Tanya."

"Oh, Emma. I'm so sorry." Anna squeezed her hand tighter. It felt good to be the comforter instead of the comforted.

Emma shook her head slowly. "I'm not even sure who my daughter's father is. I've had to live with that. I've had to answer my sweet girl's questions about her father."

Emma's voice faltered, but she swallowed hard and went on. "I know our circumstances were very different, Anna, and I'm truly not trying to one-up you with my story. It's just that I do know some of the questions you're facing now—questions about the mixed feelings you have for the child you're carrying and the hard choices you're facing about your future and this child's. Abortion wasn't really an option for me. It wasn't legal then, of course, and I didn't have a dime. And besides, I didn't know which man to go to for help. I'm so grateful now that it *wasn't* a choice. I'm afraid I might have taken the easy way out, and oh, what I would have missed! Anna, you must make Paul see what a mistake that would be. You must!"

She looked at Anna intently, and her voice became fierce. "You know my life hasn't been easy, but my daughter is the joy of my life. All my children are blessings, of course, but Tanya...she's somethin' special. The boys have been through some bitter times. Being deserted by their father at such a tender age did a number on them. But the good Lord has brought us through it all. There were times I thought we wouldn't make it, times I doubted I'd ever find happiness, but it's all been redeemed, Anna."

"I know," Anna admitted. "I knew how you felt about your kids from the first time I met you."

Emma nodded. "To see all three of my kids in happy marriages, raising my grandbabies for the Lord... I guess what I'm trying to say, Anna, is that as terrible as this seems—no, as terrible as it *is* for you and as difficult as it must be for Paul—there is hope. If I have anything to offer you, it's hope." She squeezed Anna's hand hard before letting go. "I know you well enough to know that you live your life for the Lord. Let Him carry you through this, child. Let Him be glorified. I *know* He can bring something beautiful out of even a devastating situation like this."

Anna put her head on the cool flat surface of the desk and sobbed. Her tears were not for the sorrow she was being asked to endure. Nor were they tears of self-pity. They were tears of gratitude—thanksgiving for the hope she knew had always been there, that was hers for the taking, but that God had chosen to reveal through the words of this beautiful friend who sat beside her.

She lifted her tear-stained face to Emma and threw her arms around her friend. And over Emma's shoulder, she turned her face heavenward and offered thanks there as well.

Because of the Rain

Eleven

As the days wore on, Paul treated Anna with kindness and a gentle sweetness. Yet, he was somehow distant from her, too, preoccupied with the weight of coming to terms with their situation. He took long walks alone in the evening and came home in a self-absorbed silence that Anna could not seem to break through.

Sometimes he retreated to his office. When she tiptoed by the open doorway, it tore at her heart to see him bowed over his open Bible on the desk, anguish in his posture. Often he came to bed long after she'd fallen asleep. And though his politeness rarely faltered, they spoke of little of consequence.

One evening she was cleaning up the kitchen after supper when Paul called out from his office. "Can you come here, Anna? I want to show you something."

Curious, she dried her hands and went to stand in the doorway of his office. He was sitting on the low sofa, his Bible spread open on his lap. He patted the place beside him, and she came and sat, nestling in the crook of his arm. The reading lamp on the end table beside them cast a warm glow over Paul's face, and Anna thought she saw a new light in his eyes.

"Listen to this, babe." There was an almost childish excitement in his manner as his fingers scanned the column of words. Then, in a whisper wrought of emotion, he read from the Psalms.

"For you created my inmost being; you knit me together in my mother's womb. I praise you because I am fearfully and wonderfully made; your works are wonderful, I know that full well. My frame was not hidden from you when I was made in the secret place. When I was woven together in the depths of the earth, your eyes saw my unformed body. All the days ordained for me were written in your book before one of them came to be."

He closed the book and looked up at her. Tears glistened in his eyes, but they veiled eyes full of peace, not pain. "When I read this tonight, Anna, I saw the baby we lost—just like you told me that night—so perfectly knit together, so 'fearfully and wonderfully made'—and I realized that this baby you are carrying is no less wonderfully made. The circumstances are difficult, yes, but still, God made him, Anna. I understand that now. And God has already written his days—or her days"—a smile flickered across his face—"in His book. If that's true—and I believe it is—how could we possibly destroy this life?"

Anna sat silent beside him as he marveled aloud. "In these past few days, God has searched my heart in ways that have nearly done me in. I don't know when I've ever been in such turmoil. And yet, in a strange way, it's been wonderful to be chastened by the God of the universe." He said it with awe in his voice.

"Oh, Paul…" Her throat was too full to speak.

"I'm not sure I can explain it to you when I don't understand it myself, but finally, tonight, I feel at peace. It overwhelms me that I can feel this calm when our lives are in such upheaval, and yet I *am* at peace, Anna. It's as real to me as you are beside me now."

Her heart sang hearing these words from his lips. She knew at that moment that they would have this baby. And may God help them all.

—∞—

Anna went through the next weeks with a quiet assurance in her soul. She treasured a deep feeling of trust that she would somehow be carried through the weeks and months to come. Since the night Paul had come to terms with their plight, Anna felt constantly surrounded by love, buoyed up with hope. She could not have endured it in her own strength, but with Paul's gentle caring, Emma's knowledge and empathy, and God's sweet comfort, Anna knew the hope she felt was real.

Still, at times the unknown lurked like a shadow behind every thought of peace. Anna willed the specter away, but it manifested itself without warning, sometimes gripping her with fear in the middle of the night, or while she was driving alone on the freeway. At those times, she could only cry out to God, her prayer sometimes no more than an utterance of His name.

Jeremiah 29:11 became her watchword. "For I know the plans I have for you… Plans for good and not for evil, to give you a future and a hope." Anna knew the words were for her. She had lived as a Christian long enough to know that God had a wonderful way of redeeming even the most horrible circumstances. But she had also lived as a flesh-and-blood woman long enough to know that the patience required for waiting to find just how He would perform the miracle was not always easy to summon.

—∞—

Kara and Kassandra came home for Memorial Day weekend, and though she dreaded it, Anna knew there was no avoiding telling the girls the news of her pregnancy and revealing the painful decisions she and Paul faced.

Kassi immediately burst into tears and as soon as she could, she retreated to the bedroom that still held her childhood belongings. Anna went to check on her and worried about her silence. "Don't worry about me, honey," Anna told her. "We'll get through this." She wished she felt as confident as she sounded.

Kara had her own very strong opinions about the dilemma, and a million questions for her parents. There were no easy answers to those questions. Still, Kara quickly drew her own conclusions and made it clear that she thought Anna should have an abortion. "I'm not saying I think it should be an easy choice, but Mom, if ever there was a good reason for abortion, this is it."

Still strong with the conviction that had overwhelmed her as she remembered her miscarriage, Anna shared the story with her daughters—including the remembrance of the tiny perfectly formed fetus, so unmistakably human, so unmistakably *life*.

"That would have been your sister, Kara," she said firmly.

"This is not the same, Mom. You were young. Dad was the father of that baby and—"

"That's not my point. This is an innocent baby, a precious life, just like that one. Why should this baby be punished for something it had no part in." Instinctively, she put a protective hand over her belly.

"But why should *you* be punished, Mom? You're just as innocent..." She shook her head and shrugged, clearly frustrated trying to make her point.

"No," Anna whispered. "You don't destroy a child for the sin of its father."

"But you'll destroy this child far more by bringing it into the world, than if you just end it." Kara's voice rose with conviction as she went on. "What kind of a life do you think this child would have, Mom? How could it possibly come to terms with this situation? It seems to me that sparing the child from the kind of life it would face would be the most compassionate thing you could do. Besides, I know you believe that it would go to heaven anyway. How could any life on this earth ever compare with that?"

"I do believe the baby would go to heaven if… if I aborted him. But I can't play God, Kara. I just can't believe that God has put the decision of life or death in human hands. Certainly not in my hands." She shuddered to think she'd once wanted to make that decision.

Kara just shook her head. They let the subject drop, but again and again throughout the weekend, Kara dredged it up, hounding her parents with questions and arguments. Anna knew her older daughter well enough to know that they had a continuing battle on their hands, but in a way, Kara's constant questions served to solidify their decision, to fully answer in their own minds the hard questions she posed. As they sought those answers, Anna, and Paul as well, became all the more confident that they *were* doing the right thing.

On Sunday afternoon, while Paul napped, she and her daughters sat in the sunny dining room sharing mugs of tea. Sitting across the table from her daughters, Anna marveled, as she had many times, that two sisters could be so different. Physically the girls looked so much alike that they were often mistaken for twins. But the similarities stopped at the pale blond hair and brilliant green-blue eyes, so much like their father's. Now their conversation demonstrated their very different personalities.

Cautious, inane talk about the weather and their college classes ended when Kara blurted, "Mom, what will you tell people when you start to show?" She pointed in the direction of Anna's still flat stomach. "You know you'll have to have an explanation. I mean, it's not like you two would *plan* to have a baby at your age. Are you going to tell people the truth about this—that you were raped?"

Anna stirred her tea self-consciously, caught off guard by her daughter's candor. "We just don't know yet. I guess a lot will depend on whether we decide to… to keep the baby." Just speaking the words made it seem such a senseless possibility. And yet, she and Paul had talked about the option. In fact, it was the only option they had seriously discussed since the day they had realized that abortion was out of the question. Now, voicing the idea to her daughters, it sounded absurd. They were talking about a child here. They were contemplating a commitment that would span the next two decades. *What are we thinking?*

"You can't seriously be thinking about keeping it, Mom!" The incredulity in Kara's tone reflected Anna's thoughts. "You guys would be…"—she did some quick math—"in your sixties when this kid is in high school! It'd be like Grandma Marquette trying to raise a teenager!"

Kassi piped up, quietly defensive of Anna. "Women have babies in their forties all the time, Kara. It's not that big of a deal. Besides, Mom is a young forty-five."

"She might be a young forty-five now, but sixty-something might as well be seventy." Disgust tinged her voice.

Kara was exaggerating, yet, somehow, despite the gravity of her daughter's anger, it tickled Anna to hear Kara talk like this. She could well remember when she herself had thought forty was ancient. Strange how time changed your perspective on age.

Momentarily, she forgot the seriousness of the discussion. "You know," she said, "Aunt Liz was almost forty when Matt was born." She looked at her daughters and fired the question at them. "You don't think she's ancient, do you?"

Her sister, Liz, was five years older than Anna, but she was the youngest-at-heart woman Anna knew. In truth, Matthew, now a charming ten-year-old, had helped keep Liz young. Liz's other children were grown and married, and she was expecting her first grandchild any day now. Still, thanks to Matt, she was up on the current slang, could challenge any kid on the block at the latest video game, and knew how to dress young without looking ridiculous. Anna knew her girls had immense admiration for Liz and didn't see her as "fifty-something" at all.

Kassi picked up the defense for Anna. "That's true, Kara. Just look at Aunt Liz. You'd never know she was as old as she is."

Anna laughed at the well-intended compliment, and her heart clung to the grain of hope she'd been offered. It was true. It didn't seem strange at all to imagine Liz and Dave with a young child. Why couldn't it be the same for her and Paul?

But Kara wasn't backing down. "That's different, and you know it. Besides, Aunt Liz wasn't even forty when Matt was born. Mom is already pushing fifty, for crying out loud!"

Anger flashed through her. Kara acted as though this pregnancy had happened because of Anna's foolishness or carelessness. Like she was an irresponsible, pregnant-and-unwed teenager.

Pushing her chair back from the table, Anna spoke, her voice pitched high with anger and emotion. "For your information, I am barely forty-five years old—hardly pushing fifty. And I didn't *choose* this pregnancy, Kara. You act like I did this on purpose!"

Though she was upset and near tears, Anna heard her words the way they must have sounded to her daughters—accusing and defensive. But she didn't care. She needed Kara's support. Why couldn't this daughter—just once—love her and uphold her and try to understand what she was going through. She was enduring the struggle of her life, and Kara sat here practically making fun of her!

Unable to hold the tears back any longer, Anna stumbled over her chair and ran down the hall to the sanctuary of her bedroom.

She heard the girls murmured voices and went to the door to eavesdrop. Kassi must have started to follow her because Kara said, "Wait, Kassi. Let her alone for a while." She hesitated and finally mumbled, "I'll apologize later."

"Oh, Kara! This is like a bad dream!" Kassi sounded near tears. "Poor Mom! And we're making it worse for her. What is wrong with us?"

"You don't mean us, Kass. You mean me. Why don't you just say it?" Kassi sighed, and her tone became contrite.

"I know. I know I'm probably being selfish. I don't mean to sound cruel, but this is *embarrassing*. What am I supposed to tell my friends. I mean, here we are, supposedly living in the age of enlightenment. There are solutions to these kind of things. How do I explain to my friends that my mother is *pregnant?*"

"Kara, until we know what Mom and Dad are going to decide—what they're going to tell people—we can't say anything anyway. So it's not even an issue right now. But when they do decide, I guess…well, if they aren't ashamed to tell the truth about this, we shouldn't be either. Actually, the truth would probably be the easiest thing to tell. At least then people will sympathize with us…with them …" Her voice trailed off.

"Yeah, instead of thinking they've lost their marbles," Kara said sarcastically.

"Kara, if they tell the truth—about the rape, I mean—and then decide to keep the baby, how is he going to feel when he grows up? I mean, things like that get out no matter how hard you try to keep the secret."

"They *can't* keep this baby! It would be crazy!"

Anna could just picture Kara looking at her sister as though *she* were crazy for even entertaining the idea.

"Can you picture Mom and Dad with a baby? I mean, think about it, Kass! No, they *can't* keep this baby."

—⟶—

When the girls left on Monday night there was a cold but

polite silence between Kara and her mother. Kara hugged Anna before the two sisters got into the car and drove off, but her embrace did little to assuage the great sadness Anna felt for the breech between them.

Anna knew Kassi felt caught in the middle—understanding Kara's opinions, yet feeling sympathy for Anna's predicament and having a fierce devotion to her mother.

For most of the weekend, Paul had avoided his daughters and withdrawn into silence, even with Anna. She longed to know his thoughts, to know the demons he was wrestling. She so desperately needed to confide in him, to vent her emotions with him. Especially after the difficult conversations with Kara.

And yet, she realized that her tragedy had placed him in the middle of an intense personal struggle. *If only he would talk to me.* He was probably wracked with guilt over his feelings toward the child she was carrying, over his seeming inability to comfort her. She knew he felt some responsibility for the rape itself. And now Kara's strong opinions had forced him to choose sides between his wife and his daughter. In some ways, Anna thought his pain might be greater than her own. But she knew her husband well enough to know that only in his own time would he open up to her.

And so she waited, forced to be content with their now shared conviction that this baby would be born, and forced to be content with Paul's politeness and his vague replies to her hesitant questions.

—m—

On the last night of May, Anna sat at the dining room table, textbooks and papers spread out around her, a cup of coffee growing cold in her hands. The semester was drawing to a close, and she was grateful for the busyness and even the stress she felt studying for finals. It was a relief to bury herself in her books and, for however brief a time, to push out all the questions that hounded her. She adjusted her reading glasses on the bridge of her nose and struggled to concentrate on the page in front of her.

Paul came in from the den where he had been watching an old war movie on television.

"Are you ready for a break?" he asked.

She looked at him questioningly, but pushed her chair away from the table and set her coffee cup on its saucer. "Sure."

"Let's go for a walk. We're wasting a gorgeous evening cooped up in this house."

She stood, stretched her arms over her head, then kneaded the muscles in her neck. "Mmm... it feels good just to stand up. I could use a break." She looked at her watch. "Is your movie over already?"

"No. But I couldn't concentrate. I...need to talk to you." He motioned toward her books. "Are you sure you have time? I know I'm interrupting your studying..."

She waved away his apology, sensing his openness after so many days of being distant from her. "I don't care. I'd much rather talk to you. Let's go." She reached out to him, and he took her hand and led her out the back door.

The warm brisk wind of the afternoon had died to a gentle breeze, and a full moon illuminated the street beyond the bounds of the street lamps. They walked hand in hand, in silence, Anna waiting anxiously for him to speak.

Finally he took a deep breath. "Anna, I know I've kind of checked out on you these last couple of weeks. It hasn't been fair to you and... I'm sorry. Please forgive me. I realize how selfish it's been for me to clam up like this when you need me most."

She shrugged, not wanting to stop the flow of words.

He put an arm around her and squeezed her shoulder. "I'm having a hard time with all this. I know that sounds selfish. You're the one who's been through the horror of it. You're the one who's suffering, but...well, I have to be honest with you."

He looked at the sidewalk and shook his head, and Anna feared she would lose him to the silence again.

But when he looked up at her again, the dam broke. "Anna, ever since that night we got the call from Dr. Blakeman, I've been trying to make this pregnancy real in my mind. But it just seems impossible." His words picked up steam. "I can't picture you pregnant. I can't imagine what we'll tell people... what we will tell the child someday."

She didn't miss the implications of that "we will."

"I don't know if I can love this child, Anna. We'll both be in our sixties before he's grown. I'll be almost seventy when he graduates from high school. I don't mind telling you that terrifies me. *Terrifies* me." His voice was a gruff whisper now.

Sensing he still wasn't finished and not wanting to stop this flood of honest feelings, she kept silent.

They walked on, and after a while he spoke again. "If we do keep this baby, I think we need to decide very carefully exactly what our story will be. I know how much you hate dishonesty, but if we are truly thinking about raising this child ourselves, I don't see how we can make your...*rape*"— he choked on the word—"public knowledge. But we'll need to have a story—for the child's sake."

"Do you want the child to believe you're his father?" she asked quietly.

He shook his head, looking confused. "I don't know, Anna. I'm not sure I can love this child in a way that would be fair to him—knowing that he is fully yours...and not at all mine. And I don't know that it would be right to deceive a child—a child who will someday be a man or woman entitled to the truth about their family history. I'm not sure I could have forgiven my mother if she hadn't told me from the beginning that Dad wasn't my real father. I think...it would have devastated me to have suddenly found it out when I was older."

She nodded, agreeing with him. "No. It doesn't seem

right to withhold that information from a child."

"And yet, how in the world do you make a little boy or girl understand these things in a way that doesn't reflect on them. I don't know, babe. I've thought of nothing else in the past weeks, and the only thing I know with certainty is that we can't abort the baby. Everything else is a big question. I don't seem to have any answers...."

"Oh, Paul..." She leaned against him as they walked farther from their house. "There are so many hard questions. I've been thinking a lot about what you just said—that the baby *is* fully mine. That has made it easier for *me*. It's the only way I've been able to bear the thought of going through with this. That, and the knowledge that the baby is innocent. But I realize that very fact makes it even harder for you..." Her voice trailed off, and she was quiet, collecting her thoughts. Finally, she said, "I've tried to put myself in your shoes, Paul, as much as it's possible to speculate on such a thing. How would I feel about a baby that was fully yours and some other woman's? Not at all my own? If you were to ask me to raise such a child, I don't know what my response would be. But I know it would be more difficult than what *I'm* being asked to do now."

"Well, you're right. You *can't* speculate on the reverse, Anna. Not without implying guilt on my part. That's just the nature of things. And that's what makes it a bit easier for me. The baby's not the only innocent one in this scenario. *You* are innocent, honey. That's not difficult for me to grasp."

His voice grew strong, conviction building as he spoke. He patted her belly lovingly—her stomach still firm and flat, belying the secret it cradled. "Anna, this little life is part of *you*. How can I not *love* it? If my dad could love me the way I know he did"—Paul meant Albert, the only father he'd ever known—"then I... I guess I can find it in myself to learn to love this child."

Tears sprang quickly to her eyes. She was profoundly touched by the words her husband had just spoken. They came from his heart. And Paul had a good heart. How different she'd have felt had they been conjured up because they were the right words to say or because she'd forced him to say them. But she knew intimately the sincerity in his tone, and she was filled with love for this man, whose integrity of character spilled out even in his anguish. Maybe especially in his anguish.

She stopped walking. The street was deserted, the houses along the avenue mostly darkened at this late hour. Unselfconsciously she put her arms around him and pulled him close. They stood swaying together on the sidewalk. She relished the comfort of his arms, the security of their love for each other.

"Paul?" She murmured into his shoulder. "Can we just wait? Can we not say anything to anyone, not decide anything for a while except what we've already decided—that this baby *will* be born…and loved? Maybe a month, or a few weeks at least, will give us time to get our bearings…time to pray about it… to think it all out."

He held her at arm's length and looked at her, shaking his head. The teasing inflection that was so *Paul* was in his voice now. "I've gotta say, babe, it's not like you to be willing to wait on *anything*." He smiled, and then suddenly turning serious again, he said, "I think that's the wisest thing we could do. You amaze me, Anna." He hugged her close and stroked her hair. "We'll wait then. We'll give it to God, and we'll wait on Him for an answer."

Because of the Rain

Twelve

$\mathcal{A}$nna breezed through her finals with confidence and with straight A's. She'd always been a good student, but it surprised her now to feel an almost childish pride in the grade report that came in the mail. Paul laughed at her boasting, but she knew he was proud of her, too.

School came to a close, and the warm afternoons and cool evenings of early June gave way to summer's sweltering heat. Anna was happy to be home, happy to be through with the daily trip to the campus and the constant pressure of studying.

Late in June, they quietly celebrated their 24th wedding anniversary at their favorite restaurant. Over the years, it had become their anniversary tradition to take a "How Do I Love Thee?" and "How Would I Change Thee?" inventory of sorts. They always spent the evening together in gentle marriage work—each giving voice to dreams for the future, playfully delivering their pet peeves, and then numbering the qualities they loved so about each other.

Tonight, though, the future was too frightening to speculate on, and the pet peeves seemed trivial in the shadow of the ordeal that loomed before them. Paul did try to enumerate the many ways he loved her. But Anna sensed he felt deep sadness in speaking the words, as though he were saying goodbye to some elusive part of their love.

Sitting across from each other in the dark restaurant, Paul reached for her hand and held it to his cheek, obviously too moved to go on. Candlelight played across his face, and she felt a tear slip down her cheek, thinking of what this might cost them as a couple.

"Let's go home," she mouthed, dabbing at her eyes with the linen napkin from her lap.

He nodded and placed several bills on the table, then took her hands and pulled her up. They left barely-touched dessert plates and brimming coffee cups and walked arm in arm to the parking lot. It was a bittersweet evening, but it held, at least, the gift of the knowledge of their deep love for each other, their commitment to walk through this storm together.

—◇◇◇—

The days of summer passed languidly. Despite the extra hours the summer schedule gave Anna to think, a strange peace continued to pervade her being.

Still, there were difficult moments.

Paul's mother had quietly asked Anna how she was recovering from her ordeal—meaning the rape. It was a thoughtful, innocent question, but so hard to evade truthfully.

She didn't lie to Shirley. Her answer—"I'm doing fine, Mom. Some days are better than others, but I'm going to be okay."—was the truth. But of course, it wasn't the *whole* truth.

When Paul had called their friend John Vickers from Orlando on the night Anna was raped, John and Brenda, out of true concern, had called the prayer chain at their church.

They'd been vague, only saying that Anna had been attacked, but still, an answer had to be given to mutual friends who'd heard about Anna's brief disappearance and the assault. Anna was grateful that most of those calls of concern had come before she and Paul knew about the pregnancy. Later, in confidence, Paul had told John and Brenda about the rape. Others were left to draw their own conclusions.

Paul and Anna socialized with the Vickers as couples, but Anna and Brenda rarely spent time together without their husbands. It made things easier now, having Paul as a buffer on the occasions when they enjoyed social get-togethers. But Anna knew that she'd subtly withdrawn from all of her friendships.

Even with her friend Maggie Ryan and with her sister, Liz—usually her most intimate confidante—she'd put up an emotional fence, making excuses to avoid getting together. She heard the hurt in Maggie's voice when, making feeble excuses, she refused one lunch invitation after another. She knew—hoped, even—that Maggie would eventually leave the ball in her court and quit calling.

Anna and her sister had always been very close, but until she knew how this would all end, she wouldn't saddle Liz with the awful burden of their secret. So in all her relationships, she steered conversations gingerly away from any topic that hit too close to her experience, and she deftly avoided letting any conversation become too intimate.

Emma Green was the exception. Emma had become Anna's confidante and counselor. And now that school was out, they were even more free in the friendship, no longer restrained by the conventions that discouraged teachers and students from becoming close friends.

With misplaced guilt, Anna felt almost as though she were being disloyal to Maggie and to Liz by confiding in Emma instead of them. And yet, she was so grateful the Lord had put Emma in her life at just the right time.

Emma called her several times a week to see how she was

faring. They eased into a standing lunch date each Wednesday, and Anna guarded that time like a hard-to-obtain appointment.

One afternoon while they lingered over coffee and dessert in a nearly empty restaurant, Anna told Emma of the decision she and Paul had made to wait—to not make any decision for a while.

"I don't know if I could be that patient," Emma said, amazement in her voice. "But I *do* think it's a wise decision. This isn't something that can be hurried. I admire your patience."

"Oh, Emma, three months ago, I *couldn't have* been this patient. But the Lord has given me a measure of trust in His timing, in His sovereignty, that is truly supernatural."

Emma nodded. "I can see the peace on your face. I don't understand it, but I can see that the anxiety is gone and there is a quietness in your spirit. I know the Lord has His hand on you. I know He's going through this with you, but I'm sorry... I'll never understand how He could allow it to happen." She clucked her tongue. "Why, oh *why*, did He allow you not only to go through the horror of being raped but also to become pregnant? And when there are so many couples in this world who would give anything to have a baby! My Tanya and her husband tried for nearly seven years to get pregnant. It just doesn't seem right. It doesn't make sense!"

She stopped abruptly, then held her hands palms out in apology. "Oh, Anna, I'm sorry. Here I am questioning God, while you sit there in the worst of circumstances, filled with His joy and peace! I don't understand it."

Anna smiled. "I don't understand it either. That's what's so wonderful about it." Anna stirred her coffee and picked at the last bites of cheesecake on her plate. Then she broached a subject that had been going through her mind with regularity over the past weeks. "I've been thinking a lot lately about...adoption." She watched Emma's face for a reaction, but her expression didn't change.

Anna sighed and went on haltingly. "In some ways, I think it might be harder for me to put the baby up for adoption than it would be to raise it. But I want to do the right thing. And the truth is, if I take myself out of the picture and just lay the simple facts out on the table, I think—I'm almost *afraid*—that adoption may be more of an answer than either Paul or I have been willing to admit. Especially for this child's sake."

She felt her emotions close to the surface as she voiced these ideas aloud for the first time. She enumerated her reasons on slender fingers. "I'm forty-five years old, Emma. Paul is forty-seven. I know it's not unheard of to have a baby at our ages, but I don't really think it would be best for any child. This child will have so many other obstacles to deal with. Then there are the circumstances, of course. Somehow it seems that adoptive parents could avoid the details of conception, the...*rape*"—she still had trouble saying the word— "more easily than Paul and I would be able to. I don't know if an adoption agency would require that fact to be revealed, but I don't think Paul and I could hide it from a child—at least not after a certain age. And ironically, the age that one can make a child understand what rape is would be precisely the time he would probably begin to struggle with the adoption issue itself. At any rate...adoption has been on my mind a lot lately... a lot."

Emma placed a warm hand over hers. "Could you give the baby up, honey? I mean, could you really give the child up and live with that decision for the rest of your life? Knowing you had a child out there somewhere? A child of your own body?" Emma shrugged. "I'm asking because I'm not sure *I* could."

"I'm not sure." She took a sip of cold coffee. "I hate the unknown. I hate having something to hide. You know that. But if I knew it was the right thing... if I knew for certain it was what the Lord wanted for us—and for the baby, then, yes. I think I could do it."

The waiter came to clear their dishes, and pour more coffee. They were silent until he was out of hearing distance. Then Emma asked, "Have you considered open adoption?"

"You mean where we would know the couple who adopted the baby?"

"Yes. Not only know them, you could choose them. That's how Tanya and Daniel adopted their little boy. Daniel was working for a man whose niece became pregnant out of wedlock. He knew about Tanya's struggles with infertility and knew that his niece had decided to put her baby up for adoption. She was only sixteen, poor girl. The kids hadn't really considered adoption at that point. They kept hoping for a miracle…Tanya so wanted to experience being pregnant. But adoption turned out to be their miracle. It was an answer to prayer. Oh yes, little Justin is definitely an answer to prayer." " She chuckled, obviously thinking of her grandson. "

"Oh, Emma, that's wonderful. I've heard you talk about Justin, but I never knew the story behind his birth."

"Honestly, I sometimes forget he's adopted. He's only two and a half, but he's part of our family now. He's no different than my own flesh and blood."

"I wish I knew more about the process. Where to even start."

"You'd go through a private lawyer, I think, rather than an agency. At least the kids did. Open adoption seems like it might be easier, at least from *your* perspective. You wouldn't always have to wonder what happened to the baby. You could keep in contact with the adoptive parents. Tanya sends Justin's picture to his birth mother every year on his birthday and lets her know how he's doing. They've agreed that when he's older they will let him make the decision about whether to meet her or not. But they won't have to track her down or always wonder what she's like. They already know her."

Emma folded her napkin into a triangle and laid it on the table. "It's something to think about, Anna. It would be a way to be assured that the baby was in a good home. A Christian home. One you approved of. And they'd have the baby's medical history and genetic information…well, yours at least. It's just a thought. I hope I haven't overwhelmed you."

It was a thought that haunted Anna for days. And the more she thought about it, the more she felt that it might be the answer they had been praying and waiting for. She felt certain Paul would be open to the idea as well, but she didn't want to rush him. She wanted him to have time to think things through, to pray about their decision, the way she'd been free to do since the night they'd agreed just to wait.

Just to wait. Over and over in the following days she opened her Bible to Isaiah 40:31. "They that wait upon the Lord shall renew their strength; they shall mount up with wings as eagles; they shall run, and not be weary; and they shall walk, and not faint." She let the promise seep into her spirit. And like the words of the song, she prayed, "Help me, Lord. Help me to wait."

—⁂—

All through the hot month of July, Paul and Anna enjoyed a closeness that contradicted their circumstances. In the evenings, they walked together through their neighborhood and took impromptu picnics to the park on the weekends. With Kassi working in Urbana over summer vacation, this was the first year that one or the other of the girls hadn't been living at home. In some ways, Anna felt like a newlywed.

She'd always felt healthy and energetic during her pregnancies, and this one was no exception. After the few short weeks of morning sickness in the beginning, she had begun to feel her old self again and many times wondered if she actually was carrying a child. It still seemed unfathomable to her. And her body was an accomplice to the deception. She simply didn't *feel* pregnant. She had to force herself to acknowledge that she was going to give birth—and this pregnancy wasn't going to have the happy ending her others had.

She and Paul discussed her pregnancy only in elusive terms. He was especially protective of her, as he had been when she was carrying their daughters. He wouldn't allow her to lift anything heavy, and he guarded carefully against her overexerting herself. But there were no joyful musings about what this child would be like, no arguing over names for the baby-to-be, no happy shopping trips choosing furniture and wallpaper for a nursery. Yet, most of the time, it wasn't an uncomfortable evasion of the subject—merely a fulfillment of their agreement to wait on the Lord for an answer.

And so they waited. And one day early in August, they both knew the time had come to talk again. To take the next step.

As he always did, Paul had accompanied Anna to her monthly doctor's appointment. After a twenty-minute wait in a waiting room full of pregnant young women, Dr. Blakeman's nurse led them to the small examination room and handed Anna a gown and sheet and left the room. Anna slipped out of her dress and quickly tied the hospital gown behind her neck. She felt self-conscious in front of Paul. No longer could she deny the changes in her figure. Almost overnight, her belly had rounded and firmed, and her clothes now stretched tautly over her disappearing waist. For several weeks, embarrassed by her changing figure, she'd been changing clothes in the bathroom or hurriedly in their bedroom before Paul came into the room. She shared her body with him only in the darkness. Soon, she would have trouble hiding her condition beneath even her loosest fitting clothes.

She had begun to feel stirrings within her belly that she remembered vaguely from her previous pregnancies. She remembered the excitement these flutterings had brought before. Now they only brought home the reality of the pregnancy, of the child growing inside of her.

The nurse weighed Anna and took her blood pressure and other vitals, and they waited in silence until the doctor came into the room. Dr. Blakeman had seemed sympathetic and supportive of Paul and Anna's choice to carry the pregnancy to term. Anna felt comfortable with him, trusted his expertise and discretion. Paul rose and shook hands with the doctor now.

"How is everything going?" Dr. Blakeman asked.

Anna was sharply aware of the sympathy in his voice. His question was asked with pity, as though her condition were terminal. Anna appreciated his compassion, yet for some reason, it annoyed her and made her feel defensive for the child she was carrying. "I'm feeling fine... No problems."

"Good, good." He skimmed her medical chart. "I'd like to do a sonogram today. You're familiar with that procedure, I assume?"

"I've never had one before," Anna said. "I guess that wasn't something they routinely did when I was pregnant with the girls, but yes, I know what it is."

Dr. Blakeman explained the procedure and told them that many potential abnormalities and other problems could be diagnosed and possibly averted using this diagnostic tool.

"Usually we can tell the sex of the baby by this point," he told them. "No guarantees, of course, but I'm about ninety-five percent accurate so far this year," he smiled.

The technician came in and set up the ultrasound machine on the cart beside them.

"I guess I should ask," the woman said hesitantly as she began to roll the ultrasound device over Anna's belly. "Do you want to see the images on the screen? Or would you rather not?"

Anna looked to Paul, who nodded with a shrug. He came to stand beside her at the head of the examination table, facing the small video screen. An unmistakable shape came into focus on the black-and-white screen. The technician pointed out the baby's head, the clear outline of the body, arms and legs, tucked up close to the body. Even tiny fingers were barely visible on one extended hand. And then the little heart. The tiny organ pulsated rapidly on the screen. The tech silently positioned the stethoscope and searched until she found the heartbeat. A swift whooshing sound filled the room, magnified by technology that had been new and even experimental when Anna had been pregnant before.

She watched the screen, listening to the sound of new life with astonishment. She turned to Paul and saw in his eyes the same awe that she was feeling. There was no denying this life—this *child*. Indeed, the time for waiting was over.

—ɯ—

Paul brought the car around to the clinic entrance, and Anna came out to the curb to meet him. He leaned across the seat and opened her door. She got in the car and fastened her seat belt low across her belly. She felt a new protectiveness for the little life she was carrying.

Paul drove to the far end of the parking lot, and then, without explanation, he backed into a shady parking space. He cut the engine and rolled the window down against the afternoon's oppressive heat. He turned in his seat to face Anna. "I guess it's time to make some decisions, isn't it?"

She smiled wanly and nodded, understanding. She grasped for words. "Paul, seeing the baby on that screen today has made everything so terribly real. This might be even harder than I've imagined, but lately I've been thinking a lot about adoption. It seems that everywhere I turn, I'm hearing that word, hearing it in my mind like a message or something. I know… I know how hard it would be to hold a baby—*my* baby—in my arms, and then …" Her voice broke as the reality of what she was saying hit her.

Paul stroked her cheek with the back of his hand. "*Can you do that? Can you give this baby away?*" His words were gentle, and the compassion in his voice, in his touch, soothed her. And yet, his very question let her know that he, too, had entertained the thought. And she suspected he'd merely been waiting for her to voice the idea.

"You've been thinking about it too, haven't you?"

"Yes. I have, Anna. But I didn't know if you could do it. I couldn't ask you to do something you might regret for the rest of your life. I wanted it to be your idea." He pulled a handkerchief from his pocket and wiped the sweat from his brow, then reached out to grasp the steering wheel in front of him.

He hung his head, and a long moment passed before he spoke again. Finally he sighed. "I am still willing to keep this child and raise it as my own, if that's what you want. I mean that. It won't be easy, but I do mean it." He looked at her now, questioning in his eyes.

"Oh, Paul. If I were twenty-five, or even thirty-five, if we could somehow take away the stigma of the rape for the child's sake, if we didn't have to tell anyone, I think I would want to raise this baby. I'm sure I would. But there are just so many hurdles that I don't think we can get over." She told Paul about her conversation with Emma, about the idea Emma had planted regarding open adoption.

"There's just one huge problem, Paul." She looked down at her burgeoning belly and smiled at her own unintended pun. "I'm not going to be able to hide this much longer. If we give the baby up, I don't want people to know about it. At least not now. I'm not ready to make it public knowledge yet. I have too much to work through myself first."

"But, how do you propose to hide something like this? For four more months? You can't become a prisoner in our home for that long."

"I don't know. I guess...I'd have to go away somewhere."

"Go away? What are you talking about? Where could you go?"

"I don't know." She shook her head and shrugged helplessly. "I haven't thought that far ahead. Maybe to Liz and Dave's?"

"Anna, no! What are you thinking? That's three hundred

miles from here! I couldn't get that much time off from the agency—not now with the trade show coming up and the new Bryant account."

"I didn't think you'd go with me," she said quietly.

The meaning of her words sank in, and he exploded. "Anna, I am not going to be without you for four months!" To her surprise, his voice broke, and tears sprang to his eyes. "I am not going to send you away like…like an unwed teenager. That's no solution at all! What would I tell people? *No, Anna!* I won't have that. I won't let you go!" He put a fist to his mouth.

His agony broke her heart, and she put her face in her hands. He reached for her across the car's console, and she fell into his arms. They held each other and wept.

And in the sweltering heat of August, in a nondescript parking lot in Chicago, they both realized that, despite their protests, they had been given their answer.

And for a season, that answer would wrench them from each other's arms and would test their love as it had never been tested.

Thirteen

Anna let the phone ring at the other end for the tenth time before she finally hung up. She'd been trying to reach Emma all weekend. They'd had lunch together just last Wednesday, and Anna didn't remember her friend mentioning any weekend plans. But she only had Emma's home phone number, so no other way to reach her. Now, on Sunday evening, darkness was just beginning to silhouette Chicago against a purple August sky, and Anna was feeling desperately lonely.

She wandered aimlessly through the house, picking up half-read books and magazines, then putting them down before she'd comprehended a single paragraph.

Paul had flown to Cincinnati on business yesterday morning, and he wouldn't arrive back in the city until Tuesday afternoon. With the realization that they were soon facing a long separation, they'd parted with a mutual melancholy that contradicted the short run-of-the-mill business trip. Paul had called her from Ohio three times already. Ordinarily, Anna hated long-distance conversations with him. He was usually all business on the phone—calling only to check in, not for chitchat—and she always hung up feeling a bit depressed and slighted. But this weekend their conversations had been filled with whispered endearments. Paul had reassured her of his love over and over. He'd complimented her and flirted with her as he had when they'd first fallen in love. She would have loved it had their situation been different.

Most times she almost looked forward to these short weekends of solitude. It was nice to have a few days free from any schedule but her own. Now, she felt a little lost without her husband. She picked up the phone again and dialed Emma.

On the fourth ring, Emma's low voice came across the line. "Yes? Hello?" She sounded out of breath.

"Oh, good. You're home."

"Anna! I just walked in the door."

"I know. I've been trying to call you all weekend."

"Oh?" There was concern in Emma's voice. "Is everything okay?"

"I'm just lonesome. Paul won't get home until Tuesday afternoon, and I was just wanting somebody to talk to. Is this a bad time?"

"Land sakes, no. I was hoping somebody would call so I could relive my weekend." She laughed.

"Relive? Sounds interesting. So tell me about this incredible weekend." Anna played along with Emma's playful hinting. Already she could feel her spirits lifting at the sound of her friend's voice.

"I decided on the spur of the moment to drive up to New Haven to see the kids. We had such a great weekend. And the weather was perfect." Emma chuckled, almost to herself. "That little Justin! He is just the cutest thing on the face of God's green earth."

"Sounds to me like a proud grandma talking," Anna teased.

"I'll have you know I am not one bit prejudiced. Someday I'll introduce you to that child, and then you'll see what I mean, girl."

Anna smiled as the dialect of Emma's girlhood crept into her voice. She always felt privileged when Emma slipped into the familiar, endearing jargon with her. Anna knew that it signified a good-natured, teasing intimacy, and a trust that was precious to her.

Emma recounted her trip to the small Indiana town—a suburb of Fort Wayne—where Tanya and Daniel lived. She related her three-year-old grandson's latest antics, and Anna laughed as much at Emma's telling of them as at the anecdotes themselves. It felt so good to share genuine amusement.

Emma's laughter trailed off, and her voice softened. "So how are you doing, Anna? Really?"

Anna told Emma of the decision she and Paul had made.

"I know I haven't really dealt with the fact that I'll have to go away. I'm not even sure where I'll go. I'd thought at first about my sister's. Liz and Dave live in St. Louis, but they have a ten-year-old son, and it just doesn't seem fair to subject him to all of our drama. And, of course, we want our situation to be confidential. I suppose there'll be no getting around telling our families eventually, but I don't want to be a burden to them. All I know for sure is that I can't stay here. Paul… Paul isn't taking that part of it too well. He—" Her voice broke. She missed him so much in just two days. How were they ever going to survive a separation of several months? She swallowed hard and went on. "He knows there's really no other answer, but, of course, that doesn't make it any easier."

"Oh, Anna. I can only imagine how difficult this must be. You are so blessed to have a husband like Paul. You two are strong together, and I know you'll make it. But my heart goes out to you. I'll be praying for you—both of you—every minute."

"I know you will. Thank you."

"What can I do? You know I want to help."

"Emma," Anna said abruptly. "There *is* something I

Because of the Rain

would really like your help with."

"Anything. You know I mean that." Emma waited, her silence rife with curiosity.

Anna attempted to be businesslike now, keeping the emotion from her voice. "Do you think Tanya would be comfortable talking with me about their experience with open adoption? Paul and I feel that is definitely the route we want to take, but I don't know where to begin. I thought maybe Tanya could at least give us a place to start."

"I'll call her tonight," Emma said decisively. "Daniel and Tanya are both very straightforward about Justin's adoption, and I feel certain she'll be more than willing to talk with you. I think she has a couple of books on the subject, too. Would you like me to have her send those?"

"I'll take anything I can get. Thank you. And thanks for keeping me company tonight."

"Hey, it was real torture having to tell you all about how cute my grandson is," Emma teased.

"I'll remember that the next time you start bragging, Grandma!"

Anna hung up with a smile. How would she have ever made it through this ordeal without this friend God had put in her life?

—⁂—

Two hours later she'd just crawled into bed when the phone rang. She picked up the receiver, expecting to hear Paul's voice on the other end.

"Anna, I hope I didn't wake you?" It was Emma.

"No, I just turned in." She thought she heard excitement in Emma's voice, and she waited expectantly.

"I called Tanya tonight to ask her to send those books?" Her inflection made the statement a question.

"Yes?"

"I don't know why I didn't think of this when I talked to

~ 120 ~

you before, but... well, just listen to this..." Excitement rose in Emma's voice. "Daniel and Tanya have an apartment in their basement that they rent out to college students. It just so happens that the girl who was staying with them dropped out of school and moved back home last month. They were going to use the time before next semester to do some painting and repairs. But when I told them about your situation, they offered for you to come and stay in the apartment."

"Oh—" Could it be that easy?

"It was *their* idea, Anna, and they both were immediately enthusiastic about it." Emma hesitated. "I hope you won't take this wrong, but Tanya and Daniel have been financially supporting a crisis pregnancy center ever since Justin was born. They have been praying for a more tangible way to be involved, and...I guess usually I think of crisis pregnancies involving young unmarried teenagers, and I don't want to make you feel like a charity case, but— Oh, for heaven's sake, Anna... I'm afraid I'm sticking my foot in my mouth from here to Sunday. I hope I'm not making it sound like—-"

"It's okay, Emma," Anna interrupted, trying to put her friend at ease. "I certainly think my pregnancy fits in the crisis category."

Emma sighed, then hurried on to tell Anna more about the offer. "Daniel and Tanya feel that it would be a small way they could return the blessing of Justin's adoption. And he's still young enough that an explanation about your situation won't be a problem like it would be with your nephew." She stopped abruptly. "I'm sorry. I haven't given you a chance to get a word in edgewise. What do you think?"

"I'm overwhelmed. I'm not sure what to think. But—it sounds perfect. Of course, I'll have to talk it over with Paul. How far is New Haven from here?"

"About a hundred and seventy-five miles. It takes me just under three hours to get there. I know that must sound like halfway across the world, but it's really not a bad drive. Paul could drive up on the weekends. The apartment is really small—just one bedroom—but it's fixed up real cute and it's already furnished. I think the sofa in the living room is a sleeper, so there'd even be room for your daughters to stay if they came to visit."

"Oh, Emma, this sounds like an answer to prayer. I'll talk to Paul tomorrow and let you know as soon as possible."

"There's no rush. You take your time. I know it's a big decision, and like I said, they weren't going to rent it out until next semester anyway. Well, I won't keep you, but I was just too excited to wait till morning."

"Thank you. Thank you so much, Emma."

She turned out the light and whispered a prayer into the darkness.

—⚈—

When Paul walked through the door Tuesday afternoon, Anna rushed into his arms and they greeted each other as though he'd been gone for a year. She thought wryly of the many times she'd wished for a little more passion, a little more romance in their marriage. Now she yearned for things to get back to normal—longed to get off this roller coaster of emotions and back to the luxury of taking each other for granted.

While Paul unpacked his bags, she sat on the side of the bed and told him about Emma's phone call and the offer of a place to stay in Indiana. "It's far enough away that I wouldn't have to worry about running into anyone I know, but it's close enough that you could visit often. I really think it's an answer to prayer, Paul."

As she recounted the details, she watched him hopefully, half expecting him to dismiss the suggestion without consideration. But instead, he listened intently to the details she gave him, interrupting with questions that seemed to indicate his openness to the offer.

Finally, he put the empty luggage in the back of the closet, sat down beside her on the bed, and drew her into his arms.

"Anna, I've fought the idea of your going away." He hung his head, as though composing his thoughts carefully. When he finally spoke, there was resignation but strength, too, in his voice. "You are such a part of me, and I didn't see how I could ever bear to let you go away—especially under these circumstances. But God dealt with me while I was in Cincinnati in a way I'm not sure I can explain. He gave me peace about giving you up for these few months, about you being able to get along without me for a while. I guess I'd like to think that you truly couldn't live without me." He gave a sheepish smile.

"Oh, Paul." She put her arms around his neck. "I don't *want* to be without you for even one day. You know that."

"I do know, babe. But I also realize that God's grace is sufficient to sustain us both, and I know this offer of an apartment is confirmation of that." He hugged her so tightly it left her breathless. Then, his voice faltering, he whispered, "Anna, I will miss you with everything that is in me, but I think this is God's answer, and I won't fight it."

He tipped her chin, turned her face to meet his gaze and, with an attempt at lightheartedness, told her, "We have a date every weekend. Do you understand? Don't make any other plans."

She laughed through her tears, and the baby in her womb stretched and somersaulted as if to remind her of his presence.

Because of the Rain

Fourteen

Two weeks before Anna was to go away, she and Paul drove together to New Haven to meet Daniel and Tanya Walker and to work out the details of the arrangement.

The Walkers lived on the outskirts of town in one of the city's newer developments. Anna liked Tanya immediately and marveled at how like her mother the young woman was. Taller and slimmer than Emma, Tanya had her mother's flawless mahogany complexion and the same warm friendliness in her dark eyes. For the first time, Anna realized that she would miss Emma almost as much as she would miss Paul. She was glad for the tie to her friend that Tanya and Daniel provided, and she hoped Emma would visit often in the weeks to come.

Daniel Walker was a quiet man, but as introductions were made, Anna sensed his warmth. He extended a well-muscled arm and grasped first her hand and then Paul's in a friendly welcome. Emma had told them that Daniel was in his mid-thirties, but his wiry black hair was painted with glints of premature gray, giving him the appearance of a slightly older man.

Justin Walker was every bit as adorable as his grandmother claimed. He had a sturdy little body and a head full of tight black curls. He reminded Anna of a little man with his polite grown-up greeting. But his bright, dark eyes held a glint of mischief, which Paul easily coaxed out of him while they sat drinking iced tea on the deck in the Walkers' rambling backyard.

Paul reached out and, unseen by the little boy, quietly caught a fat June bug that had been buzzing loudly against the back screen door. When Justin turned his way, Paul held the bug out between his fingers. "Well, look at this, Justin. I must be lucky, I got a bug in *my* tea." Hiding the bug in his palm, he noisily pretended to eat it, smacking his lips as though it were the tastiest treat ever. It was a prank he had delighted his own daughters with when they were small, and Justin's reaction didn't disappoint him. The dark eyes grew wide, and his mouth dropped open. He looked questioningly at his dad, but Daniel played along with the joke.

"Didn't Mom put a June bug in your drink?" he asked his son. "Tanya," he chided, winking at Anna, "you forgot to give Justin a bug in his juice."

Tanya just smiled and shrugged apologetically.

"Well, here," Paul said, holding out the original bug to the little boy. "I'll share with you. Looks like I got two."

Justin shook his head skeptically, seeming not quite sure how to take this teasing stranger. Then, to everyone's amazement, the toddler plucked the squirming bug from Paul's hand, and before anyone could react, he put his pudgy hand to his mouth and did a perfect imitation of Paul's fake bite. The real bug buzzed back to the screen while Justin smugly chewed on a crunchy pretend insect. The adults howled with laughter. Justin just stood there grinning, enjoying his little triumph of one-upmanship.

When the evening ended, Daniel walked his guests to

their car. Tanya had said her goodbyes earlier and taken Justin off to get ready for bed. Paul stood in the driveway and extended a hand to Daniel. The younger man took it firmly in his own.

"I can't tell you what this means to us, Daniel," Paul said with emotion.

"Hey, man, we're happy to be able to help. I... I have to tell you," he stuttered self-consciously, "we... we really admire what you and your wife are doing. Not many people would go through with this the way you are—not in this day and age." Daniel looked at the ground, seeming embarrassed at his own words of tribute.

The uncomfortable moment was broken by Justin's little voice calling across the yard. "G'bye, you guys."

They turned to see him, barefoot and pajamaed, waving gaily from the front porch. Tanya waved one last time before scooping her son up and carrying him back into the house.

As they started the long drive home, Anna thought what a blessed distraction the little boy would be for her in the coming weeks.

—⁓—

Anna put off packing until the last possible minute. It hardly seemed real that she was going to pack her bags, get in the car with her husband, and not return to this house—*their* house—for several months. It was even more difficult to think that Paul would return without her.

Thoughts of what life would be like in New Haven, fears of being apart from Paul, and trying to remember all the little details that needed to be taken care of—appointments to cancel, filling the freezer for Paul, writing lists and instructions for this man who'd never had to know how the washing machine worked or where the extra light bulbs were stored—all served to help Anna put out of her mind the *reason* she was going away.

Tanya had recommended an ob-gyn in New Haven, and Anna instructed Dr. Blakeman's office to transfer her medical records to the clinic there. Aside from that small detail, she had put the pregnancy—especially the decisions that needed to be made in order to go ahead with the adoption— out of her mind temporarily. She simply couldn't deal with all of it at once.

Too quickly the days of August passed, and the day they'd set for her departure arrived. Paul helped her pack, and when she began to close the bags and assemble them near the back door, he carried each one out to the garage, methodically packing them into the back of his SUV. Anna watched him soberly.

She thought back to Kassi's tearful goodbye the week before. Kassi had come home for a long weekend before starting back to school. They made plans for her to visit Anna while she was in New Haven, and it helped to have the date to look forward to. Kara, Anna feared, would not come.

She'd not spoken with her oldest daughter since the weekend the girls had been told about the pregnancy. Anna thought they'd at least agreed to disagree on the topic. Yet, when almost three weeks had gone by without any word from Kara, Paul grew concerned and called her.

"I don't know what there is to talk about, Dad," Kara had replied tersely. "I just can't deal with this. I'm sorry. Truly, I am sorry, but I don't think this is something Mom and I can discuss anymore. I don't think there's anything else to be said." She'd refused even to say hello to her mother.

Paul had hung up, more angry than hurt. But Anna was hurt. It cut deeply to have Kara's continued rejection and disapproval. As much as she wanted to reconcile with her daughter, she simply didn't feel that she could deal with one more conflict in her life right now. She tried to put it out of her mind. Yet, how could she put her own child out of mind? She couldn't pretend it didn't matter. It mattered a great deal.

Paul had played mediator between mother and daughter.

He had called Kara and told her of their decision to put the baby up for adoption. Anna thought Kara would be relieved that at least they weren't keeping the baby. But even after this news, it seemed there'd been no softening on Kara's part. Paul still could not persuade her to even speak with her mother on the phone.

At that, Anna allowed herself anger. How could Kara be so unfeeling, so seemingly ignorant of the anguish in which she and Paul had made their difficult decisions? In many ways, the anger was easier to deal with than the hurt. It caused deep pain to realize that her daughter could forsake her at a time when she most needed her love and support.

She and Paul both feared the changes they saw in their daughter—Kara's seemingly changed beliefs on abortion and the almost haughty attitude that she wore so often now. Anna worried about what had provoked these changes. Had she and Paul failed to properly instill in their daughter the values and morals that they treasured so highly? Had they failed to pass on the very essence of their deeply held faith? These questions tortured her like thorns in her already wounded flesh.

As cold-hearted as Kara had been toward Anna, Kassi was warmth and sweetness. She truly seemed to understand the degree of her mother's suffering, and she had given Anna such reassurance of her support and her empathy. "You're doing the right thing. Mom. I just know you are," she'd told Anna more than once. The conviction in her voice had been a real comfort to Anna.

Kassi also made excuses for her sister, telling Anna, "She doesn't mean to hurt you, Mom. She *wants* to be there for you—I know she does—but I think she truly thinks she can still talk you out of having the baby. She's scared for you, Mom. Even for your life—for what you'll go through giving birth. She's seen—in her job—what can go wrong during birth."

They'd both laughed at the comparison of Anna's pregnancy to the canine and feline gestations that Kara dealt with at the animal clinic. Anna knew there was probably a small bit of truth to what Kassi said. But she felt a hot flush of shame when she admitted to herself that much of Kara's emotion was purely selfish—embarrassment for Anna's situation, impatience for the inconveniences it caused her, and probably more than anything, her stubborn need to always be right. Anna felt responsible for Kara's self-centered spirit, and she rebuked herself for failing to give her older daughter whatever it was that instilled compassion and selflessness in a child.

Though Kassi was attentive and careful with Anna, she could not hide her anticipation of the new year about to begin at the university. Kassi had finally begun to feel comfortable with campus life. She'd made close friends at school and was enjoying her studies. It was only natural that she was anxious to get back to that life. Anna knew it was wrong, but she was a little jealous of her daughter's enthusiasm, of her young carefree life. For one rash selfish moment, Anna wished she could trade places with her daughter. If only she were packing for something as exciting as going back to school instead of for the exile that awaited her.

Paul's voice brought Anna back to the present. "Honey, do you want this bag up front, or can it go in the trunk?" Paul had loaded the car in silence. Now he was down to the last few items.

It had been difficult deciding what to bring. Though the Walkers' apartment was furnished, Anna would still need everything for the kitchen. And though she wanted in no way to make the apartment feel like home, she did, at the last minute, pack a few knickknacks to set about on the coffee table and nightstands.

She carefully wrapped framed photographs of Paul and the girls, and of her parents and Shirley, and put them in the backseat of the car. She was afraid the family pictures would be constant reminders of all she had left behind, but she decided she could always pack them away if looking at them made her too homesick.

They had agonized over what to tell their families. In the end, it came down to a choice between telling the awful truth, and making up an elaborate story—telling a lie...there was no other honest way to put it. And though the truth was painful and hurtful, she simply couldn't tell the lie, couldn't keep up the pretense of any story they could have fabricated. Now, as she packed to escape all those they could not tell, she remembered with a sick feeling in the pit of her stomach the day they had told her parents.

On a sunny day, just three weeks ago, they'd driven the sixty miles to the Greysons' home in the country. Her mother had taken it especially hard. Charlotte Greyson was worn down with the burdens of caring for Anna's grandmother, and since Paul and Anna had never told her parents about the rape itself, they'd had to absorb that horrible fact at the same time as the news of Anna's pregnancy.

They'd eaten lunch together, laughing and exchanging news as though nothing had changed, as though things would always remain the same.

After lunch Anna went down the hall and helped her mother feed her grandmother and get her settled back into the hospital bed that dominated her small bedroom. Almost five years ago Grandmother Cavender had moved from her farmhouse ten miles outside of town into the Greysons' home. Her first two years in their home had been spent puttering contentedly about the large sunny rooms, helping her daughter care for the house and the large collection of houseplants Charlotte had nurtured over the years.

Now Grandmother spent her hours in the bedroom Liz and Anna had shared as teenagers. The elderly woman drifted in and out of wakefulness, mostly unaware of her surroundings, though seemingly free of pain. She had lived this way for almost two years now, ever since a stroke had left her nearly bedridden. Anna sometimes wondered how much longer her grandmother could go on like this. And how much longer her mother could continue to care so patiently for the tiny, frail woman whose years numbered nearly a century.

Her mother's days were consumed with the arduous chores of feeding and bathing her mother—each procedure such a painstaking process that she barely finished one when it was time to begin another.

The family had tried to convince Charlotte to place her mother in a nursing home, or at least to hire a nurse to come into their home. But Charlotte Greyson wouldn't hear of it. Her only concession was to hire a woman to clean the house once a week, and that was at her husband's insistence.

Anna's aunt drove from Chicago to relieve Charlotte once or twice a month, and Anna and Liz helped when they could. But essentially, Mom had committed herself to being her mother's caretaker for the remainder of the older woman's life. Anna at once admired her mother's devotion to her parent and was angered by her stubbornness in not allowing outside help to ease the burden. She knew well who Kara had inherited her stubborn streak from.

Now, with lunch finished and Grandmother napping, Anna could not put off the reason for their coming any longer. She sat beside Paul at the round oak table in her parents' elegant dining room. Across the table her parents nursed second cups of coffee. The sun cast bright patches on the lace tablecloth where the remains of a fragrant cherry pie sat in the middle of the table. The sunny bay window behind them was filled with Mom's plants, green and flowering, though a yellow leaf here and a faded blossom there hinted at neglect.

Suddenly nervous, Anna stared down into her grandmother's delicate china cup, her own coffee long grown cold. Her heart began to pound.

Jack and Charlotte were relaxed, smiling, unaware of the gravity of their daughter's visit. Anna reached for Paul's hand, which rested atop the table. He wrapped strong fingers around hers, and she sighed involuntarily.

Her parents exchanged curious glances. Paul squeezed her hand again. She felt his strength and knew his grasp conveyed his willingness to do the telling if she but asked. But for her parents' sake, she could not let the task pass to Paul. The words must be her own.

She looked into their expectant faces. "Mom, Dad, we… we have some bad news to give you."

Alarm came into her mother's eyes, and her father's smile faded, his jaw tensing. Love for these two people who had given her life surged through her. The deep lines in their faces and the strands of gray in their hair touched her in a way she did not fully understand. An emotion, new to her relationship with her parents, welled fiercely within her, and she recognized it as the same protectiveness that tore at her heart when Kara or Kassi suffered pain or disappointment.

Swallowing hard, Anna took her mother's thin hand in her own. Its coolness, the knuckles gnarled with arthritis, surprised her. She hadn't realized until this moment how much her mother had aged over the past few months.

Anna choked on tears, but she looked into her mother's eyes and hurried to tell what they had come to tell. "Mom, I want you to know that I'm doing fine. We haven't wanted to worry you, because I really *am* fine but… Do you remember when I went with Paul to Orlando last spring?"

Numbly her parents nodded in unison, waiting, she knew, for the unimaginable.

"I… I was walking alone one night, and… I was attacked…and raped."

Her mother gasped as the announcement sank in, and Anna tightened her grip on her hand. "I wish that was all of it, Mom, but…there's more."

Anna found herself directing her words at her mother. Jack Greyson was a rock of strength, and Anna knew he would deal with the news in his own strong quiet way. But her mother would need reassurance. Her mother would need convincing that Anna's words were true.

"I'm pregnant."

"Oh, Anna," her mother said, a thin but almost cheery note in her voice. "You're pregnant?"

Anna knew what her mother was thinking—hoping… She couldn't allow her to carry that hope for a moment. "Yes, Mom. I… I became pregnant when I was raped."

"Oh, Anna, maybe not. You…you don't know that. Maybe it is Paul's baby you're carrying. You don't know," her mother repeated, her voice high and pleading.

"No, Mom," Anna said firmly. "Paul had a vasectomy seven years ago. We know the baby could not be his. We know that for certain."

Paul and Anna had never shared their decision about the vasectomy with her parents. It must shock them to find out there were so many things about her—about them—that they didn't know. Even now she wasn't sure her mother understood. Anna's mother had never been comfortable speaking about such things with her children.

"We haven't told anyone except the girls, of course, and Shirley, and I will call Liz and tell her," Anna continued. "We aren't sure when—or if—we will tell anyone else. I know that makes it difficult, Mom, but…well, we don't want it known. At least not yet."

"What…what will you do, honey?" Her mother's eyes were glazed over, and her face was a mask of confusion.

When Paul explained that Anna would be going to New Haven until the baby was born, explained that they planned to give the child up for adoption, Anna knew that her father grasped everything. She knew that he would be there to convince her mother of the terrible truth of this news and, in time, to offer comfort and a strong shoulder to lean on.

Sitting together in the house that Anna had grown up in, she and Paul answered her parents' many questions and made polite conversation. Every sound seemed magnified in the silence of the house. The clock ticked loudly on top of the bookcase in the front hall. Outside the back door, the air conditioner purred like a huge, contented cat.

In a small strangled voice, Anna's mother asked them if they would stay for supper, but Anna knew Paul was anxious to get back to the city and knew, too, that her parents needed time alone together to recover from the shocking news. They said their goodbyes tearfully, without acknowledging the time that would pass before they would next see one another.

While Paul brought the car around, Anna went back to the bedroom to bid her grandmother goodbye. Grandmother Cavender lay on her back in the high bed, one bony arm gripping the side of the raised bedrail, the other clutching the neatly turned back quilt that covered her thin frame. Her eyes were closed, the lids translucent, a tracery of pale blue veins beneath the thin skin. Anna tiptoed to the side of the bed and leaned over to place a light kiss on the cool wrinkled cheek.

Her grandmother's eyes fluttered open. There was recognition in the faded brown eyes, "Well, love…your…heart, Annie," she said in the slow quavering voice that age had bestowed on her. She sighed and closed her eyes again.

Anna smiled and her heart soared. Rarely had her grandmother seemed to know her in the past two years. The words of blessing—"well, love your heart, Annie"—were old, familiar ones that held sweet memories. Now they were a gift.

"Goodbye, Grandmother… I love you," she whispered. "God bless you."

Driving away from her childhood home that afternoon, Anna felt as though a huge weight had been lifted from her shoulders. Yes, she would worry about how her mother was coping, but at least now she could be herself with her parents. This secret was too heavy to carry, along with everything else she bore.

Anna called Liz the following morning. The two sisters had always been close. Five years older than Anna, Liz had been her constant protector and encourager since the day she was born. Now her sister assumed the role once more.

"Oh, Anna, are you sure you can give this baby up?" she cried. "Have you thought about how it will be to wonder every day where that baby is, where that child is on every birthday?" Liz's first grandchild had been born in April, and Anna knew her sister had been reminded anew of the tender sweetness a baby brought.

But of course she'd thought about it. These were questions she'd asked herself a thousand times. But always, the *child's* questions seemed more urgent. She explained to Liz that she and Paul hoped for an open adoption, that they hoped to remain in contact with the adoptive parents. But of course there was no way to know yet how it would all work out.

"I know you're doing the right thing," Liz cried. "I know you are. But, oh, Anna, I just don't want to see you hurt."

They wept together across the phone lines, and Anna was comforted by her sister's response. When she told Liz that she was going to New Haven, her sister offered their home instead.

"Liz, thank you. I know I would be welcome there, and I did think about it, but... well, this isn't something Matt should have to deal with. A ten-year-old shouldn't have the burden of keeping a secret of this magnitude. And New Haven is so much closer. Paul will be able to come every weekend." Anna's voice broke as she thought anew of being without him.

Liz didn't argue with Anna's reasons, but asked, "Have you told Mom and Dad?"

Anna told her about revealing their trip to her parents' house the day before, and Anna knew that Liz would be another source of strength for their mother.

Paul's mother already knew about the rape, and she accepted this new disclosure about Anna's pregnancy with her usual strength and her no-nonsense take-charge attitude. Shirley offered to take care of Paul's laundry and the housecleaning in Anna's absence. Anna made Paul promise to allow his mother that privilege. She knew it would be good for both of them.

It seemed that the Lord was teaching her a great deal about allowing herself to be ministered to, to allow the precious people God had placed in her life to encourage and uplift her. Anna began to see the pride that had kept her silent for all these months for what it was. She was humbled—and lifted up at the same time—by the genuine caring and love offered so graciously now to Paul and to her.

It amazed her once again to see the phenomenon of God's grace in the most formidable circumstances. How many times had they felt His mighty hand shelter them in the midst of turmoil, seen great spiritual growth spring from the soil of adversity? It built up her faith in a way she could not have imagined a year ago. Someday, perhaps, she would be able to testify to that great Power. Perhaps somewhere down the road in her humble testimony an inkling of the purpose of this tragedy would be found. She found the thought comforted her.

Anna handed Paul the last of her things to be packed in the backseat of the car: a stack of books she'd been wanting to read along with her laptop and iPad. Though she couldn't exactly keep all her friends up to date on what was happening in her life these days, she thought it would help her mother and the girls if she at least kept in touch with them.

Emma had suggested she keep a journal of her thoughts and experiences. Anna wasn't sure she could do that just yet, but she had an empty notebook, just in case.

With a final glance at this wonderful house she and Paul shared, she locked the back door and went around to the passenger side of the car. Even though she felt like she was already saying goodbye, there was no need for her and Paul to say parting words yet. They had a three-hour drive ahead of them.

The landscape seemed...*dusty*, and though they'd turned the calendar's page to September, August's sultry days had not yet given way to the cool breezes of autumn, and Anna watched through the bug-splattered windshield as plowed fields and unfamiliar small towns rolled by. Though they'd driven this same route two weeks ago, she felt as though she were traveling through a foreign country. She longed for the familiar streets of their Chicago neighborhood and felt the deep pangs of homesickness already.

How will I endure the separation? Her throat tightened, and tears sprang to her eyes. Quickly she turned her head to gaze, unseeing, out her window so that Paul wouldn't see her weeping. They'd shed too many tears together in the past months. She didn't want to waste these last precious hours together on crying.

Paul turned the car off the interstate, and soon Highway 30 stretched endlessly before them.

Fifteen

They arrived in New Haven just before dark. The houses on the Walkers' winding streets were not large or ostentatious, but they were stylishly designed, and with lawns and landscaping now established, the neighborhood gave the appearance of moderate affluence.

After a short visit with Tanya Walker, Paul and Anna walked around to the apartment, and Paul unlocked the door. The faint smell of fresh paint wafted through the open door, and Anna saw that the entire apartment had been repainted since they had first looked at it.

Despite being in a basement, the space was bright and modern. The architect had designed the windows of the Walkers' basement apartment to allow in as much light as possible, and the pale freshly painted walls and beige carpeting reflected and multiplied the light.

The kitchen was open to the living room, with a small dining area to one side. The single bedroom and the bathroom were down a short hallway at the end of the living room.

The furniture was well-worn but tastefully upholstered and in good repair. Paul helped Anna put the few dishes and kitchenware in place, and together they made up the bed with the brightly patterned linens she had brought from home. She would be very comfortable here. Comfortable... and desperately lonely.

Paul sat down on the freshly made bed and pulled her down beside him. She bit her lip and fought for control as he gently took her hands in his, caressing her fingers, wordlessly tracing her wedding rings with his own slender fingers. She knew he was saying goodbye.

Anna looked up at him through wavering tears and saw that his own eyes were brimming. He took her into his arms, his embrace expressing what words could not. They stayed that way for long minutes.

Finally, he held her at arm's length and looked into her eyes. "I love you, Anna." Such simple words—three syllables they'd spoken many times a day for more than twenty years. But never had there been such meaning, such emotion behind their utterance.

He tipped her chin toward his face, his tone an attempt at lightheartedness. "Let's not say goodbye. I'll see you this weekend, okay? Is it a date?"

She couldn't speak. She only nodded and tried to smile.

Arm in arm, they walked to the door of the apartment. Paul kissed her gently and then crushed her to him. Too soon, he tenderly pushed her away and opened the door.

She touched his cheek one last time. "Drive carefully," she said, in her own attempt to make this moment seem less formidable. Then she closed the door behind him.

She heard his tires crunch on the gravel outside the high basement window, and she leaned her head against the door and sobbed.

—◁◁—

When the sun broke through the sheer curtains in Anna's bedroom the next morning, she squinted and looked around the room, trying to remember where she was.

Above her, she heard the thuds of Justin's little feet padding across the bare wood floor. It was a strangely comforting sound. She lay in bed, mulling over the events of the day before and contemplating her new life in Indiana. She felt relief that the goodbyes were over and the move had been made. In many ways, the apprehension over her impending separation from Paul had been worse than the actual event. Still, she couldn't help thinking about her husband and worrying about how he was faring without her.

She imagined him back in Chicago. He would be up and getting ready for work about now. She worried that he wouldn't remember how the coffee maker worked, that he would forget that the toast would burn unless he turned the setting to "light." Had she remembered to leave orange juice in the refrigerator, or would he need to thaw a can from the freezer? She shook her head and laughed wryly to herself. She was being ridiculous. He was a grown man, perfectly capable of taking care of himself. And she'd left a volume of notes and instructions. If he ruined his breakfast, he would just hit the donut shop on his way to work.

Shaking off her anxieties, Anna threw back the covers and headed for the bathroom. She was determined to use her time in New Haven productively. There were lawyers to confer with, a hopeful young couple to seek out. She intended to remove her emotions from the process and begin the task of finding a mother and father for her baby...no, not her baby, *the* baby. She needed to remain objective.

She showered quickly and brewed coffee to go with the muffins that Tanya had left on the kitchen counter for her. She was grateful for Tanya's thoughtfulness. Anna had brought a few staples with her from home, but she would need to stock the refrigerator before she could make a single meal. But it had been late when Paul left yesterday, and she hadn't wanted to waste their last minutes together shopping for groceries. But now, without a vehicle, shopping would be difficult.

Paul had suggested that she bring her car to New Haven, but she'd resisted the idea, not wanting to make the trip by herself or sacrifice their last hours together driving separate vehicles. The nearest taxi was miles away in Fort Wayne, and though New Haven did have bus service, it existed mostly for commuters to Fort Wayne and wasn't convenient for simple errands around the smaller town. She should have listened to Paul. She would check into rental car rates later on. She would need transportation.

While she nibbled at the muffins, she made a list of things she needed to accomplish: contact the lawyer Daniel worked for, shop for groceries, set up an appointment with the new doctor, call the car rental company, write to the girls and her parents.

She looked at the list spelled out in her neat precise printing and felt a sense of satisfaction and purpose. She would keep busy and make the best of the solitude that had been imposed upon her.

A cheerful "I love you" e-mail from Paul was waiting on her laptop and chased the remainder of gloom away. She could do this. And with God's help, she would.

—⁂—

Three days later, Anna realized with dismay that every item on her to-do list had been crossed off, and she found herself with a full day stretching before her and nothing to do. Even the stack of books she'd brought had mostly been read, and those that hadn't held no interest for her.

She wandered restlessly around the apartment, cleaning things that were already spotless, plumping pillows again and again, picking up a book to try again, but then somehow not comprehending the few paragraphs she scanned. She thought she would go crazy with boredom.

She was actually looking forward to the middle of the month when she had appointments with the Walkers' lawyer and with her new doctor in Fort Wayne. She lived for the weekend, when Paul would come.

Anna was determined not to become an annoyance to Tanya and Daniel, but the young couple seemed to go out of their way to include Anna in the family's activities.

Several times when they were grilling meat on the deck, they insisted that Anna join them for supper. They also invited her to ride with them to church on Sunday, but Anna declined, knowing Paul would still be here. Besides, she was showing quite obviously now, and she wasn't sure she could bear the stares and questions of well-meaning people simply trying to make visitors to their church feel welcome.

Anna delighted in little Justin, and the three-year-old seemed to take to her just as quickly. He remembered Paul from the Marquettes' first visit and recounted the bug-eating incident to Anna time and time again. She loved this silly remembrance of Paul and laughed genuinely with each telling of the little boy's story.

One evening when she discovered that Tanya was having trouble finding a baby-sitter for the evening, she eagerly offered to watch Justin for them.

"Oh, Anna, I couldn't ask you to do that," Tanya protested.

"Nonsense! I would love to watch him for you. My social calendar isn't exactly overflowing these days," she said wryly. "Please. This is one small way I can repay all your kindness to me. And besides, I would really love the company."

"Well, if you're sure…"

"Absolutely," Anna assured her.

The evening flew by, and she felt a sense of fulfillment at being able to help out.

Justin was an adorable little boy, unspoiled and well-disciplined, but ornery enough to keep things interesting, too.

When it got too dark to play outside she and Justin made chocolate chip cookies together in the Walkers' cheery kitchen. Justin sat on the counter, sneaking a finger full of cookie dough every time Anna turned away to search the cupboards for another ingredient. It reminded her of when the girls were small. Kara and Kassi had always loved to help her bake. As it always did, the thought of Kara brought a wave of sadness over her. She wondered what her daughter was doing tonight.

When the last batch of cookies was cooling on the counter, Anna helped Justin into his pajamas and tucked him into the low bed.

"Good night, buddy. Thanks for letting me help you with the cookies."

"You're welcome. I did good, didn't I?"

"You sure did. I think those are some of the best chocolate chip cookies I've ever eaten."

"Me too! Maybe Mommy will let me have some for breakfast."

Anna laughed. "I wouldn't count on that, but I bet you can have one after lunch tomorrow." She tucked the blankets around him. "You'd better get to sleep or I'll be in trouble for letting you stay up so late."

"Nah, Mommy wouldn't care."

"Well, just the same, you better go to sleep now."

He stuck his lower lip out, but the yawn that followed told her he was sleepy.

"Okay," he said through another yawn. "G'night, Anna."

She turned out the light and started to pull the door shut.

"Anna?"

"What, honey?"

"Do you have a little boy?"

She came back into the room and knelt beside his bed. "No, but I have two little girls. Except they're not little anymore. They grew up and went away to college."

"Oh. Do you miss them?"

"I sure do."

"They could come and live down the stairs with you." Justin always referred to Anna's apartment as "down the stairs."

She smiled and patted his cheek. "That's nice of you to offer, honey, but they both have their own apartments."

"Well, then you should get *another* kid."

Anna swallowed hard. "How about if I just borrow you once in a while?"

"Okay," he said, as if that settled it. He stretched and burrowed deeper. Anna patted the blankets over him again.

—ᴡ—

In the days that followed, she looked for excuses to offer her baby-sitting services. Tanya always protested and tried to pay Anna for her time, but Anna finally convinced her that it was she who owed them the favor.

Justin squealed with delight whenever he saw Anna, and the toddler's devotion to her did wonders for her spirits. Anna always had a funny "Justin" story to tell Paul when he called or Skyped. It was wonderful to have something to laugh about together.

Paul sent her sweet text messages throughout the day and called every evening. Anna sometimes felt homesick and depressed after she hung up from talking to him, but it was good to hear his voice and share her thoughts and her day with him.

She knew he bore the burden of secrecy surrounding her absence. Just before she'd moved to Indiana, they'd finally told John and Brenda the whole story. They knew they could trust their friends to keep this confidence, and it comforted Anna to know Paul had someone to confide in—someone who knew the truth.

But they'd told everyone else merely that she was visiting friends in Indiana. Now that Daniel and Tanya had indeed become dear friends, it didn't seem like a lie.

One evening while they Skyped, Paul confided, "I may as well tell you… I'm afraid people are drawing the wrong conclusions about your extended visit. Apparently the rumor is going around that our marriage is in trouble."

"What makes you say that?" They'd discussed that possibility when they decided to keep Anna's condition in confidence, but she'd hoped it wouldn't happen.

"Maggie has called me three times now, wondering when you're coming back. Wondering why you didn't even tell her you were going on a trip. She called again just last night…"

"What did you tell her?" she asked in a small voice.

"Well, what am I *supposed* to say when week after week people ask me where you are?"

They had a fuzzy Skype connection, but even so, she could tell by the set of his jaw that he was angry. And not at Maggie.

"I'm sorry, babe."

"I told her—again—that you're still visiting friends."

"Thank you…for covering for me. I'm sorry," she said again.

"She jumped all over me, wanting to know *who* you were visiting. She practically begged me to tell her what is going on. I stuttered around like an idiot and finally ended up telling her that you would explain everything when you got back. Then she asked sarcastically if you were ever *coming back*. I finally told her she'd simply have to wait for you to explain it all. I know that leaves you with some tough questions to answer when you do come home, but I didn't know what else to do." Paul's voice had lost its angry edge, but his jaw was still taught, and Anna knew he hadn't softened the story for her sake.

"And," he continued, "Reverend Mason called Sunday afternoon to say they've missed us in church. I told him what I told Maggie: you're visiting friends, and you've decided to stay a while longer. I feel like a fool—a liar and a fool." The anger reared its head again.

It was excruciating to have him angry at her when they couldn't mend the rift in person. And Skype was a poor substitute for being able to really look into his eyes. She remained silent at her end, understanding his frustration but not knowing what she could do to assuage it.

Finally he spoke again, his voice softer, his eyes apologetic. "Honey, of course everyone is reading more into your absence than I'm telling them. People aren't stupid. But there's nothing we can do about it. Let's just forget it. You and I know the truth. That's all that matters. I don't know what else we can do at this point. I'm sorry. I... I shouldn't have said anything. You have enough on your plate. It doesn't matter."

But it did matter. Anna could tell he was sorry for even bringing up the subject, so she let it drop. But it was something she dwelled on for a long time after they disconnected the call. Her unwillingness to reveal the whole truth, especially to her close friends, was putting her family in a very awkward position. She didn't have to answer any of the prying questions herself—she was sequestered safely away from the curious stares and probing questions. But Paul—and to a lesser extent, the girls, her parents, and Shirley—were left to make excuses and cover for her.

She suspected Paul dealt with it by simply avoiding their friends. He spent weekends with her in New Haven and came home late from work to the TV and the quiet of the house. It seemed terribly unfair—he needed his friends now especially—and yet, she simply didn't feel she could bear coming home after the birth to face the knowing glances and whispers that were certain to be there if they made their tragedy known.

But poor Maggie. Anna had purposely distanced herself from Maggie after what happened in Orlando. Though the two friends had grown apart somewhat when Anna went back to school, she still cherished her friendship with Maggie Ryan. But the truth was, Maggie could not always be trusted with a secret. And this was a confidence Anna could not afford to have betrayed.

And then, when Emma had become a confidante, Anna had let her friendship with Maggie drift further. She knew that Maggie had probably been asked by mutual friends "What is going on with Anna Marquette? We haven't seen her for weeks. And she and Paul haven't been in church…."

She could almost hear the gossip now, hear the unspoken accusations that would color the whispered questions. She knew that if the situation were reversed, it would hurt her deeply to have to admit that her close friend had not confided in her. That she was as much in the dark as the rest of them about what was going on with the Marquettes. Deliberately or not, her actions had created a deep rift in her friendship with Maggie. Could such a breach ever be mended? How many friends would she lose before this was all over?

And so, along with a child of rape, Anna carried the heavy baggage of guilt for the pain and alienation she was causing her family and her friends to endure.

Sixteen

Walter LeMans was accustomed to dealing almost exclusively with civil suits, but when Daniel Walker mentioned the dilemma of Paul and Anna Marquette to him, he agreed to meet with the couple. LeMans had handled the adoption of Justin Walker—his niece's son by birth—and found it to be such a satisfying experience that he gladly agreed to handle the process should this couple from Chicago decide to retain his services.

Anna Marquette sat alone now in front of his huge oak desk in the large well-appointed office.

"Mrs. Marquette, as Daniel probably told you, I don't ordinarily handle adoptions. That being the case, I don't have a long waiting list of prospective parents for you to choose from, but I'm certainly glad to help in any way I can. I understand you and your husband have opted for an open adoption similar to the Walkers' adoption?"

She nodded.

LeMans was all too aware that he'd been chosen by this

woman in the midst of a crisis merely because he lived in Fort Wayne and had been recommended by the Walkers. He doubted Mrs. Marquette had given a thought to the fact that his African-American heritage in large part dictated his clientele. He didn't want to make her any more uncomfortable than she already was, but he felt he needed to broach the subject. Shifting uneasily in his chair, he cleared his throat. "As you might guess, Mrs. Marquette, most of my clients are African-American. I assume that you are hoping for a white couple to adopt your child?"

"Oh, well…I …." She paused, obviously taken off guard by his question. "I guess I hadn't really thought about it. You came highly recommended by the Walkers," she explained. "But, yes, I guess my feeling is that it would be easier for the child if he were placed with parents of the same race."

"That's fine," he said, holding up a hand to reassure her. "I tend to agree with you, but I just wanted to be certain of your intentions. Shouldn't be a problem. I have a number of colleagues who practice here in Fort Wayne who handle adoptions regularly. I have no doubt that between us we'll be able to give you the names of any number of couples for interviews. I'm sure you're aware of the long waiting lists for healthy babies. And with an open adoption you will, of course, have the final say on the couple to whom your child will go."

Again, she nodded wordlessly. She seemed nervous and close to tears. He could scarcely imagine how difficult this must be for her. He thought of his own wife—Margie was just a year younger than Mrs. Marquette—and wondered how he could ever accept something so horrifying happening to her—to them. Silently, he vowed to do everything within his power to help this woman and her husband get through the difficult days ahead.

He reviewed his role in the Walker adoption with Anna Marquette, outlining the legal and financial aspects, as Daniel had permitted him to do.

"You realize there's a possibility that your particular case may be classified as an interstate adoption, especially since it is your intention to return to Chicago after the birth… Indiana has no residency law stated for adoption, per se, but I'll have to do some checking into Illinois statutes. That may change some of the time frames we'll be working with, but I'll find out about that, and we'll get started as soon as possible with some resumés for you to look at."

He explained his fee structure and gave her some documents to read and have her husband look over before signing. "Again," he explained, "the interstate nature of this case may affect some of the procedures, but since you were married at the time of the conception and birth, Indiana law automatically presumes your husband to be the father of the child. He has both rights and responsibilities toward the child, and we will, therefore, need his consent in order for an adoption to be legally sound. That shouldn't pose a problem. I assume he is willing to sign adoption papers?"

"Oh yes," she stammered. "Yes, of course. It's a decision we made together."

"Good." He steepled his fingers over his desk. "Now, I think the next thing that might help us make some headway is to make up a list of qualifications that you would like the prospective parents to meet. We've established that you'd prefer a white couple." He scribbled a notation on a yellow legal pad. "Other things you might consider: is a particular religious persuasion important? Do you wish for there to be other children in the family? Do you have objections to a prospective mother working outside the home or a father who travels a great deal?" He enumerated the list on long tapered fingers. "We'll make every effort to see that your child is placed in the kind of home you want him to be raised in."

"Do… do you want me to list those things right now?" she asked uncertainly.

"You may if you wish, or if you'd like some time to think about it and talk it over with your husband, you can bring me a list whenever it's convenient. Let's see..." He glanced over the brief notes he'd taken earlier when Daniel had presented the situation to him. "The baby isn't due until December thirteenth. Is that correct?"

Again, Anna nodded silently.

"There's no rush," he said kindly. "You take your time and make sure about this. There will always be couples waiting for babies, but you will only make this decision once. You just take your time," he repeated.

Mrs. Marquette rose to her feet. "Thank you so much," she said. "I do want to talk this over with my husband. Paul will be here this weekend, so we'll try to make some decisions, and I'll get back to you next week. Will that be all right?"

"Absolutely."

When they parted, her handshake was firm, and he thought he saw a growing confidence in her eyes. It was rewarding to know he would play an important role in helping this woman through a very difficult crisis.

—⚬⚬⚬—

Paul and Anna sat on the sofa in the apartment, stockinged feet tucked under them, legal pads spread in front of them. It was Paul's third weekend in New Haven, and they'd spent the entire time designing a composite of the perfect mother and father.

"Okay," Paul said, all business. "Read what we have so far."

Anna leafed past the early drafts of their list to the neat row of attributes they had composed. She read the checklist aloud to him with detached objectivity. "Must be devout Christians who will raise the child in the Christian faith; prefer couple who have been married at least seven or eight years, with no history of marital problems; prefer well-educated couple; must be financially stable couple; siblings okay, but not essential; prefer supportive grandparents living nearby; prefer home in a rural community or small town ..."

She looked up at him. "What else?"

"Do you think we should say something like about there being no opposition from close family members to the fact that the baby was conceived by rape?"

She hadn't thought of that. "Definitely. Oh, Paul... It would be awful if this baby was rejected by his own family." The fierce sense of protection she'd begun to feel for this growing life, reared up.

She started to add the requirement to the list. But she stopped abruptly and looked at him. "Do you think we're being too particular?" She tapped the list to emphasize her point. "At the rate we're going, you and I wouldn't even qualify." She smiled, but her question was serious.

"I know it sounds like we're asking for a lot, Anna," Paul answered, "but these aren't hard-and-fast requirements. We're just making a wish list. Maybe we could divide it into two separate lists," he mused aloud. "One listing the absolutes, the other would be things we're willing to compromise on."

Anna nodded and began writing at the top of yet another clean sheet of yellow legal paper, this time dividing the page into two separate columns. By the time they were finished, they'd concluded that the only things they were truly unwilling to compromise on were that the couple raise the child in the Christian faith, and that there be no history of marital problems. Some of the other things were more important to one or the other of them, but they decided those issues would wait until they met the couples before deciding what was acceptable and what was not.

Anna sighed and leaned her head on Paul's shoulder. Sometimes she wondered if they would ever get through this.

One thing was clear: they would not get through it unchanged.

—∽∾∾—

"Come on, Anna. Just say yes, and I'll quit bugging you."

Tanya Walker stood in the living room of Anna's apartment, hands on hips and exasperation in her voice. She had been trying to talk Anna into joining them for supper all week, and now, though Tanya's voice held teasing annoyance, Anna knew that her continued refusals were becoming truly frustrating to her generous landlady. But she felt she'd already imposed on them enough. They'd invited her to picnic with them on the deck several times during her first couple of weeks in New Haven, and she'd happily accepted those invitations. But she didn't intend to make a habit of imposing on them. She certainly didn't want them to regret having asked her to live in the apartment.

Now, Anna sighed and smiled weakly. "I really do appreciate the invitation, Tanya. Just please don't go to any trouble. You're treating me like an honored guest, and I never intended that to be our arrangement."

"Just hush, Anna. I wouldn't be asking you if we didn't want you to come. Besides, since when do honored guests spend their evenings baby-sitting free for the hosts' ornery little boy?" She gave Anna a jubilant smile that said "Aha! I got you on that one." Before Anna could argue, Tanya continued, "And don't worry, I promise you filet mignon and *créme brûlée* are not on the menu. In fact, I'll probably just toss a couple of peanut butter and jelly sandwiches and some Cheetos out on the table."

Anna laughed. "You know, that actually sounds pretty good."

"You are hopeless," Tanya snorted, rolling her eyes. She playfully picked up a small throw pillow from the couch and tossed it across the room at Anna.

In the few short weeks she'd been in New Haven, Anna had grown to love Tanya Walker. The young woman reminded her more of Emma every day. She had the same easygoing playful manner, and like her mother, Tanya made Anna feel comfortable just being herself. It was such a blessing not to have to work at being friendly and cheerful when she so often didn't feel that way. And yet, Tanya's joking allowed Anna to put her worries aside for a few minutes each day and just enjoy some plain old fun.

Tanya looked at her watch. "Oh my goodness!" she said with feigned astonishment. "I'd better get up there and get the silver polished and the crystal washed."

"Oh, you!" Anna laughed. She lobbed the pillow back in Tanya's direction, but Tanya was already halfway up the stairs, and the cushion hit the door as it closed behind her.

—⁓—

A week after Anna delivered their list to Walter LeMans's office, Daniel brought home a thick folder for Anna, accompanied by a short note from the attorney. LeMans had sent resumés of three couples for her to look over, telling her he felt any one of the couples would be excellent prospects.

When Anna called Paul that evening to tell him, she was surprised that her hands were trembling. Having actual names of prospective parents made it all so real. Here in her fingers were brief biographies of six complete strangers—and she was going to hand her baby over to two of them. She put a protective hand over her belly and sat down on the sofa in the tiny apartment to look over the papers.

Her study and knowledge of psychology made these glimpses into other people's lives intriguing. If she could just be objective about this, it would be fascinating.

The first resumé was from a couple in their early thirties, Tom and Wendy Scott. Tom was an engineer, and Wendy taught English at a private high school in Fort Wayne. Though Wendy's biography stated that she loved her job, it also assured that Tom's salary was large enough that Wendy hoped to stay home when they had children. The couple had been trying to conceive for three years, and there didn't seem to be any medical reason for their infertility. They were just beginning the adoption process, and though they had their name listed with two agencies, they liked the idea of open adoption, and for that reason felt they might have more success going through a private attorney.

As Anna read about the couple's hobbies, self-identified strengths and weaknesses, and their brief philosophy of child-rearing, it struck her that no intelligent person would state on a resumé of this kind that she had a raging temper, for instance, or that her main weakness was deceitfulness. Instead, their lists of weaknesses were couched in euphemisms intended to be perceived as strengths. Tom's weakness was that he tended to be a perfectionist. Who wouldn't want a father who strove for perfection? Wendy's statement about her weakness was "I sometimes worry too much, and am overly cautious, at the expense of not taking risks that might have positive results." It was obvious this was intended to convey the assurance that a child would be unquestionably safe with such a conscientious mother.

Though Anna knew that she herself would have filled out such a questionnaire in exactly the same way, she found herself wishing to see an honest admission of weakness, an honest assessment of human frailty. Perhaps then she wouldn't wonder what actual weakness lurked in each applicant's personality.

She glanced briefly through the other two resumés. On paper, each couple glowed. Even the attached photographs didn't give Anna a clue as to the true character of each subject. They were all well-dressed, smiling, hand-in-hand or arm-in-arm, looking happily married and stable.

By nine o'clock, Anna was too exhausted to read any more. This was too difficult. She couldn't make a decision of this magnitude on her own.

She tossed the stack of folders on the coffee table and wearily went back to the bedroom.

Seventeen

"Oh, look, Mom. Isn't this darling?" Kassandra pointed to a headless mannequin sporting a stretch-denim maternity jumper that accentuated the very pregnant figure of the model. They were shopping at Glenbrook Square in Fort Wayne. Kassi had flown into the city after her last class the day before, and Anna rented a car in New Haven and picked up her daughter at the airport.

Paul had flown out of Chicago on Friday morning and wouldn't be back until late Monday afternoon, unable to get out of a weekend conference with a client in Dallas. It was the first time since Anna had been in New Haven that he hadn't been there on the weekend. She'd dreaded the thought of a long weekend alone in the apartment, so she was especially grateful for her daughter's presence now.

After a leisurely breakfast that morning, Anna happily suggested their favorite activity together—shopping.

Now she looked dubiously at the maternity outfit Kassi was admiring. "Honey, at my age, *darling* isn't exactly what

I'm going for."

Kassi laughed and began to browse through the merchandise displayed on the racks. She picked up a simply tailored navy and white dress. "How about this?"

"That's better," Anna said, considering the possibility. She took the dress from Kassi and held it at arm's length. She squinted, trying to imagine how it would look on her. "Oh… I do like that—as far as maternity clothes go," she added sardonically. "What size is it?"

Anna had always been slim, and until now, she'd been able to get by wearing a few of her loose-fitting outfits. In the past weeks, though, her waistline had ballooned at an alarming rate.

With her other pregnancies, she'd begun to wear maternity clothes in her fourth month—not out of necessity, but because she *wanted* to announce to the whole world that she was expecting a baby. She'd loved the flowing feminine lines of maternity smocks, and they had flattered her lithe frame. Now she was grateful that until now she'd been able to hide her condition under layers of loose tops and sweaters—grateful, too, for the cooler days since she'd arrived in Indiana, which made their wearing acceptable. But there was no question that the inevitable undisguisable changes in her figure had taken place. It was time to shop for bona fide maternity clothes.

Anna hadn't seen either of her daughters since she'd left Chicago almost eight weeks ago. She had been afraid that Kassi would be uncomfortable with her now obvious pregnancy, and she'd hesitated at even allowing Kassi to come to New Haven. But the truth was, she missed the girls terribly. Both of them.

She'd secretly hoped Kassi might persuade Kara to come along. But while she hoped for that, she dreaded it too. Kara would not be able to ignore Anna's figure and the significance it held. And Anna didn't feel strong enough for another confrontation with her headstrong daughter.

Kassi had arrived at the airport alone. Anna rushed forward and hugged her tightly, struggling for composure. As she released her daughter from her embrace, she saw the look of shock on Kassi's face, as she stared down at Anna's round belly.

"Kind of hard to get your arms around me now, huh?" Anna joked.

Kassi looked embarrassed, but a smile caught the corners of her mouth. "You're big as a barn, Mom!"

Her candor had broken the ice, and they'd dissolved in laughter and walked down the concourse arm in arm, back to "normal" again. Whatever that was.

Now she and Kassi were enjoying a wonderfully close time, shopping and visiting together.

Kassi had found several outfits on sale for herself, and Anna splurged and bought her daughter an expensive pair of running shoes. Now they were shopping for Anna. She was determined not to spend a lot of money on this necessary but short-lived wardrobe, and she'd already found several pieces that would work together well and that weren't too terribly expensive.

She tried on the navy dress and was pleased with Kassi's genuine compliments. Anna and Paul had begun going to church with Daniel and Tanya on Sunday mornings, and it would be nice to have something new to wear. She added the dress to her purchases, and mother and daughter walked back through the department store toward the entrance that opened into the enclosed mall.

As they passed the department store's cosmetic counter, a heavily made-up young woman stopped them. She wore a black smock over stylish designer jeans, and her russet hair was a mass of lacquered curls. She carried a basket brimming with colorful pamphlets and small vials of cologne.

"How are you ladies today? Would you like to sample our fragrance special of the week?" Before they could respond, she hurried on with her well-rehearsed, animated sales pitch.

"This is a wonderful fragrance for that special man in your life. It's called *Apres Midi* and has a clean citrus scent with woodsy undertones. Now this is available in several forms. The sample I'm giving you ..." Ceremoniously, she handed each of them one of the glass vials attached to a leaflet picturing a muscular male model posing by a forest stream. The young woman continued with her spiel. "Now this is the cologne, but we also have after-shave and a body splash available if you prefer."

They thanked her for the samples and hurried away, exchanging smiles over the girl's dramatic presentation. When they were out of hearing distance, Kassi opened her vial and waved her hands in a snippy imitation of the salesgirl. "A clean citrus scent with woodsy undertones," she singsonged as the cologne splashed out of the vial. "Ugh! This stuff is awful!" She gave a comical grimace.

When the cloyingly sweet scent reached her nostrils, Anna felt sick to her stomach. Strangely terror-stricken, she stopped abruptly in the middle of the mall concourse, struggling to catch her breath and shake off the panic that rose in her throat.

Kassi had gone several steps before she noticed that Anna lagged behind. In a voice still filled with teasing laughter and feigned impatience, she called, "Come on, Mom. You're slowing us down. There's shopping to be done."

Anna tried to croak a reply, but she was afraid she was going to throw up.

"Mom? Mom!" Kassi's voice rose to almost a scream as she saw Anna.

She rushed back to Anna's side and took her by the arm. "Mom, what is it? You're white as a sheet! What's the matter?" Kassi's voice shook.

Anna couldn't reply. All she knew was, with no warning she'd been transported back to Orlando. She might as well have been back in that shadowed alley where she'd been attacked and violated. She felt the same smothering terror she'd felt when the rapist had thrown the coarse cloth over her face.

Trembling, she looked into her daughter's face, trying to reassure her that she was all right. But she wasn't sure it was the truth. Maybe she was just having a panic attack. But what had precipitated it?

She let Kassi lead her to a wooden bench a short distance down a side corridor of the mall. She sat down beside her, a protective arm around her mother's shoulder.

Kassi leaned close and studied her. "Mom? What's wrong? Is it… is it the baby? You've got to tell me."

There it was again. That sickeningly sweet odor. Anna looked at the open vial of cologne still clutched in Kassi's fingers. And she knew.

She'd smelled that same pungent odor the night she was raped. She hadn't remembered that detail until this moment. *He* must have been wearing this same cologne. She read the tiny print on the vial: *Apres Midi.*

"Oh, Kassi. It's that smell! It's…that cologne." She buried her face in her hands. "I think the man who…raped me was wearing that same scent. I'm sorry, honey… it just… it just took me back to that awful day. I'm sorry," she whispered, struggling to get it together for Kassi's sake.

Kassi quickly gathered up the samples and threw them into a nearby trash receptacle. But she tucked one of the pamphlets bearing the manufacturer's address into her purse. Then she rinsed her hands under the icy stream of a drinking fountain, shaking them dry and sniffing her fingers to be sure she'd washed away every trace of the scent.

She watched Anna all the while, and at the sight of Kassi's worried expression, she willed herself to stop shaking.

Kassi came back to the bench and sat down beside her. "Are you okay now?" Her voice was high and gentle, as though she were speaking to a child.

Anna nodded. "I'm sorry. I… I don't know why I let that bother me so much. It… it just took me by surprise. I hadn't remembered it till just now. It's so strange how a simple odor can bring back a memory... a... a horrible memory." She shook her head and rubbed her temples with her fingertips. "I'm fine now. Really. Please, let's just go."

"Mom, I think we should tell someone about this."

"Tell who, Kassi? What would that accomplish?" Her voice sounded angry in her own ears. Her anger wasn't directed at Kassi. She simply wanted to forget this incident. She didn't want to talk about it anymore.

"Mom, if this guy has raped before, someone else might have noticed the cologne. You said you hadn't remembered it till now, but it could be evidence."

Anna hadn't thought of that. In the months since the attack, Paul had called the Orlando police only once to ask if they had any leads in the case. There'd been nothing to report, and Anna had been almost relieved at that news. She doubted they would ever catch the guy. She'd felt safe again in their friendly neighborhood in Chicago, and here in the small community of New Haven—both far from Orlando and the horror of that night.

Now, she just wanted to put it all behind her. She didn't want to think about having to come face-to-face with that monster in a police lineup, or in a Florida courtroom. *She didn't want him found.* She didn't want to put a face on the monster.

But she appeased Kassi with a vague agreement to tell Paul about the incident when she talked to him next.

Their shopping trip spoiled by the incident, they drove back to New Haven in a heavy silence.

When Paul called from Dallas that afternoon, Kassi answered the phone. She didn't give Anna a chance to tell him—or avoid telling him—about the upsetting incident. She related the whole story to her father in detail, spelling out the name of the cologne and reading the address of the manufacturer over the phone.

Anna could tell by Kassi's long pauses and the solemnity in her voice that Paul was taking the incident seriously, probably copying the information down on the notepad by the phone in his hotel room. She was certain he would call Orlando as soon as he hung up from talking to her.

She wished they would all just forget about it. In the back of her mind, she nursed a fear that she would forever be subject to flashbacks like she'd had in the mall today. How many other little details had she put out of her memory? What other little pieces of that violent night were lurking in her subconscious, ready to jump out and betray her at the least little trigger—a smell, a taste, a timbre of voice? Even a mild French accent from some character on television had sickened her since that fateful night.

—⚊—

Sunday evening, Anna saw Kassi off at the airport. She came back to the empty apartment feeling empty herself—sad and depressed. She could hear Daniel's and Tanya's laughter above her and Justin's happy squeals. She longed to join them, to be part of a family on this lonesome night. But she knew how precious the Walkers' weekends were to them, and she didn't feel right barging in on their family time more than she already had.

When Paul had called from Dallas that afternoon, she'd spoken briefly with him while Kassi was still there. But they hadn't been able to speak intimately. Now she tried to reach him on his cell phone, but there was no answer. He'd likely taken his client to dinner and wouldn't be home until late.

She tuned the radio to a classical music station and turned the volume up high enough to muffle the voices upstairs. She let the melancholy strains of a violin overtake her, and she sat weeping on the sofa, torturing herself with memories of other days—of her own family, together and happy, before this terrible thing had torn them apart.

She allowed herself an hour of self-pity, and then she switched off the radio, hung her new clothes neatly in the closet, and crawled into bed.

That night, for the first time in weeks, she dreamed again of the tall man in the shrouded face chasing her, closing in on her in the dark alley while the skyscrapers of Orlando towered above.

Eighteen

When Paul came to New Haven the first weekend after the episode with the cologne, Anna feigned fatigue. They stayed in the apartment, going over the resumés Walter LeMans had sent and watching brainless sit-coms on television.

Anna saw the concern in Paul's eyes Sunday morning when she begged off going to church—what had become the highlight of her week—but she couldn't reassure him. Despite all her efforts to deny it, the incident in the mall had frightened her, and she found herself withdrawing from even the meager social life she'd established in New Haven.

The following Monday, she holed up in the apartment again, ostensibly reading through the resumés yet another time. But having only herself to fool, she finally tucked the folders away in a dresser drawer, pulled on a heavy sweater, and started out on a walk through the neighborhood.

Daniel and Tanya's neighborhood boasted curving sidewalks and walking paths. The afternoon was beautiful—sunny with a brisk breeze blowing through the wooded acreage.

Though it was early November, the trees still clung to their gold and crimson finery, and the crisp rustle of leaves filled the late autumn air. Anna felt more invigorated with each step she took.

She rounded a curve and came upon a small playground. A young mother sat on a bench near the sidewalk, rocking a tiny infant back and forth in a stroller.

"Hi there." The friendly red-haired young woman waved a freckled hand at Anna as she passed by.

Anna couldn't resist stopping to admire the baby. She bent down and peered into the stroller. "He's adorable. How old is he?"

"Two weeks old today," came the proud answer. "Looks like it won't be long till you'll be pushing a stroller too. When are you due?" She smiled knowingly at Anna's round belly.

Anna almost cringed at the question. "In December," she answered quickly, hoping the conversation would end there.

"Oh, just a few more weeks. Is this your first?"

Anna could sense the woman's curiosity. Though Anna knew she looked good for forty-five, she also knew that she didn't look like a typical first-time mother. She felt self-conscious now and tugged at her bulky sweater in an effort to keep it from clinging to her stomach and emphasizing her condition all the more.

Panic rose within her. She didn't want to explain her situation to a complete stranger. As her pregnancy advanced and she and Paul became "regulars" at the church in New Haven, Anna had shared her situation with a couple of the women in the congregation and with the pastor, but there had been no reason to tell anyone else. There was no one else in New Haven that she knew well enough to tell.

Now she managed to stammer, "No. No, it's not my first. We… We have two daughters…" With an awkward wave, she hurried on down the path.

Her own voice sounded rude in her ears, and she saw the look of disappointment on the young mother's face. But she walked on briskly until the playground was out of sight. Anna remembered the isolation she'd felt when her daughters were babies, remembered the courage it took to reach out and make friends. She felt ashamed at the rejection she must have made this new mother feel. She had become so self-absorbed in the past weeks, thinking only of her own feelings, her own troubles.

Taking a deep breath, not certain what she would say, but determined to apologize for her rudeness, she circled back toward the park.

The young woman was still there. She had taken the baby out of the stroller and was loosening the ties on his little cap. He squirmed and squinted against the sun's brightness. His mother turned his face away from the sun and noticed Anna approaching. She smiled hesitantly.

"Hi," Anna said, apology already in her voice. "This might sound strange, but I'm sorry if I seemed rude a few minutes ago."

"Oh, that's okay. You weren't exactly rude. I guess I'm just a little overfriendly sometimes. My husband would call me snoopy," she said sheepishly and gave a little laugh.

"Oh no. It wasn't that. It's just…" Anna motioned to the empty space on the bench. "May I?"

"Sure… Of course." The young girl moved the baby's diaper bag to the ground, and Anna sat down beside her.

She sighed heavily and plunged in. "You see, the circumstances of my pregnancy aren't exactly happy. I wasn't sure what to say to you."

"Oh? I'm sorry…" The girl looked at Anna expectantly.

"I'm not looking for sympathy. Please don't think that. I just want you to understand why I seemed so unfriendly. My husband and I have two grown daughters. This baby I'm carrying is the result of— Well, I was raped."

The young woman gasped. "Oh, no. I'm so sorry."

Anna held up a hand. "No, please… It's okay. We are going to place the baby for adoption, and everything is working out. It's just kind of difficult to have my circumstances be so obvious." She glanced wryly at her belly. "I didn't want you to think you'd done anything wrong."

The girl smiled, suddenly shy, and extended her hand. "I'm Gina," she said.

Anna shook her hand warmly. "Hi, Gina. My name is Anna." She looked at the baby, now sleeping in his mother's arms. The sunlight played on glints of strawberry in the downy hair on his head. "Would you mind if I held him? I don't want to wake him," she said hesitantly.

"Oh, don't worry," Gina laughed, tossing her red curls behind her shoulder. "Nicholas could sleep through a tornado." Gina transferred the infant awkwardly to Anna, working around the mound of her belly. The baby felt sweetly heavy in her arms, but his weight was a comfort that filled a need deep within her.

She held the baby while he slept for almost an hour, relishing the warmth and life he represented. She and Gina spent the rest of the afternoon in quiet conversation, bound by the ties that motherhood seemed to bestow on all women.

Walking home, Anna breathed a prayer of thanks that once again God had shown her His loving care. This time through a flesh-and-blood angel with curly red hair and freckles.

—∞—

Paul came for his usual weekend visit, and Anna presented him with the stack of resumés, now six deep. It seemed that every few days, Walter LeMans sent home another folder with Daniel.

After spending the majority of the weekend poring over the biographies of potential adoptive parents, Paul and Anna quickly eliminated one couple on the basis of their liberal philosophy of disciplining children, and another couple because they already had two children. Though Anna hoped this child would eventually have a brother or sister, there were so many couples who could not have children at all. She'd decided she wanted this baby to be a much-appreciated, much-longed-for blessing, and she reasoned that her baby would be more so to a childless couple.

They decided to interview two couples and hold the other two resumés in case neither of the first interviews worked out.

Anna set up the appointments, and Paul took a Friday off the second week in November.

When they arrived at Walter LeMans's office for the first interview, the young man and his wife were already seated in front of the attorney's desk. They jumped to their feet and acknowledged the introductions.

Their conversation with the couple came easily, and Anna felt comfortable with them immediately. Yet something—something she could not quite put her finger on—troubled her. Marilee Conwell was extremely attractive and equally well-dressed. Her shoulder-length black hair was immaculately styled, each wave perfectly sprayed in place. She was friendly and poised, yet the more they visited, the more Anna perceived that Marilee wasn't genuine. She seemed overly concerned with money, with the status and material things it could buy.

Anna liked Marilee's husband, Steve, but before the interview was over, she'd dismissed the Conwells as a possibility. Perhaps she was being too picky. Such an interview was bound to put even the most unflappable couple on edge. Perhaps she needed to give them another chance. But when the interview had ended, and Anna asked Paul's opinion, he voiced the same concerns she'd felt.

Paul sighed. "I'm afraid that young woman has no clue what an upheaval a baby would bring to her perfect house and her perfect wardrobe."

Anna knew that their refusal would be a disappointment to the Conwells, but Paul's concurrence put to rest any qualms she had about rejecting them. Their decision was not a personal affront. The child's interests had to be foremost in their decision.

The next interview was scheduled for later that afternoon.

Paul and Anna walked across the street and ordered coffee in a nearly empty restaurant while they waited for the appointment time. Quietly they reviewed the resumé of the couple they would be meeting, and together they formulated the questions they wanted to ask.

They waited in the attorney's office for several minutes, making idle conversation with him until the next couple arrived.

They look so nervous, Anna thought as the couple awkwardly took chairs across from them, *and so terribly young.* Yet, Anna knew from their resumé that Matthew and Jeanine Whiteman were both in their thirties. Anna felt almost embarrassed at the amount of personal information about each couple that she and Paul had been privy to. The Whitemans had been trying for almost ten years to have a baby. Jeanine had been diagnosed with endometriosis, but she'd managed to become pregnant twice. Sadly, each of those pregnancies had ended early on in miscarriage. There was pain and sorrow etched on each of their faces.

The Whitemans' resumé, like the others, had been accompanied by photos. But the couple looked nothing like their pictures. Jeanine Whiteman was much prettier than her photo revealed. She had pale blond, naturally curly hair and a lovely smile that lit up her entire face. Anna liked her immediately.

Matthew was much taller than Anna had supposed, and while his photo made him look confident and gregarious, in person, the man was so shy it was hard to imagine how they would ever get to know him. He spoke haltingly and looked often to his wife as though she was coaching his responses.

Nevertheless, Anna felt good about him. He wasn't rude or sullen, just painfully shy. This whole process must be very difficult for him.

The law offices had closed for the day, and a maintenance crew had assembled noisily in the hallway outside the attorney's office. After introductions had been made all around, Walter LeMans suggested they go down the hall to a conference room. "I think we'll all be more comfortable there," he said, gesturing toward the commotion outside his door.

They filed down the hallway and seated themselves at a long table in the large room. Paul and Anna sat side by side across the table from the Whitemans, with Walter LeMans at the head of the table.

LeMans opened a folder, which he had carried from his office, and spread its contents in front of him. Formally repeating the same words of instruction he had used in the earlier meeting, he said, "Well, I'm sure you've all read everything there is to read about one another. This is the time to ask any further questions you might have. I'll try to answer them to the best of my ability. We'll start with you, Mr. and Mrs. Marquette." He nodded to Paul.

Paul cleared his throat, then looking directly at Matthew, he smiled and said, "First of all, please call us Paul and Anna."

Anna silently blessed him for trying to put the quiet young man at ease. Matthew murmured his thanks, and his wife quickly interjected, "And you may call us Matt and Jeanine, of course."

Paul glanced at the folded papers in his hand. Anna knew he didn't really need a reminder of the questions they had, but he unfolded the papers nevertheless.

"Matt, Jeanine," he began, looking at each one as he spoke their name, "we feel very positive about the things we've read in your resumé. I guess one issue that we didn't see addressed was that of the baby's conception. As you are aware, this child was conceived as a result of rape, and we're concerned that there might be some adverse feelings about this." He held up his palm. "Not that we think either of you would be guilty of that, but we're thinking of other family members. We would like reassurance that this issue will never be used against the child. We know that sometimes people can be very cruel."

Anna nodded her agreement with Paul's concern. They both waited for a long minute. When Matthew looked up, his voice was full of emotion, but it was strong and sure.

"Mr. Marquette—Paul, Jeanine and I have decided that it would serve no purpose for anyone to know that the baby was conceived in rape. When the time comes, we will tell him the truth—that we do not know who his father is. If, at some point when he's older, he asks us more specifically, we won't lie to him. But we do not feel that it's necessary for our families or anyone else to have that information."

Jeanine spoke up. "We didn't put this in our resumé because we wanted a chance to explain our reasons to you. It seems that since you don't know the father's identity, there would never be a question of the child trying to look up his father. There won't be a family history, a medical record, that sort of thing. It…well, like my husband said, it doesn't seem to serve any purpose to tell him anything except that we don't know who his father is."

Paul ran a hand over his freshly shaven face. "There's only one problem I see with your plan, and it would come a ways down the road, but still, I think it needs to be addressed. Our idea of an open adoption means that we will keep in contact with you. We don't want there to be the mystery that sometimes confuses adopted children, especially as they enter their teens. We want you to always know where we are, so if at any time this child wants to meet Anna, that option will be open to him or her."

Anna interrupted to clarify. "I hope you understand that we would never try to contact the child without your consent. But I would …" She swallowed the lump that had formed in her throat. "I would very much like for you to send pictures of the child and keep us informed about his health—that sort of thing. But I promise you that this would be *your* child. We wouldn't interfere in any way." She looked at Paul, trying not to break down.

It seemed so incredible that they were here in this room, saying these words that would change their lives forever. She put her hand lightly on Paul's knee. "I'm sorry, honey, I didn't mean to interrupt."

"No, no. I'm glad you clarified that. The point I was trying to make is that since it is possible that the child may someday make contact with Anna, it doesn't seem fair for her to bear the burden of answering questions about the father. If you give an adopted child the name of his birth mother, but tell him that his father's identity is unknown, eventually he will arrive at one of two conclusions: either his mother was raped, or she was promiscuous. I certainly don't want Anna's virtue questioned in that way."

"Oh my!" Jeanine's face flushed, and her husband looked at the floor.

"I'm so sorry." Matt said quietly. "We hadn't thought of that."

Again Matt was silent for a long time. He seemed to be a man who did not speak before thinking. *A good quality*, Anna thought.

When he finally spoke, he asked, "Would it be acceptable to you if we did not disclose the fact of the rape to anyone except the child...and not, of course, until he was older? We'd give him the choice of who or whether to tell at that time. We would not give him his birth mother's name— Anna's name—until he knew about the rape as well. Would that be agreeable to you?"

Paul looked at Anna, questioning. Her mind raced. It seemed like a reasonable solution, but she needed to think it through. "I think that sounds quite fair, but please, I'd like some time to think it over."

"Of course," the Whitemans answered as one.

The couple voiced their natural curiosity over the vague information they did have about the birth father. Paul relayed the information to them, and Anna was gratefully aware that he was making it all sound as matter-of-fact as possible. It was painful for her to listen again to even this vague account of the rape.

They visited casually then, each seeming comfortable to voice concerns and raise questions. The atmosphere was very cordial and polite, but warm, too. Matthew Whiteman began to open up, and it was plain that the two couples liked each other. No small thing, Anna thought.

After an hour, Walter LeMans, who had sat mostly silent throughout the meeting, stood and extended his hand to Paul. "Paul, Anna, I think we've probably covered as much ground today as we can." He turned to the Whitemans. "I'll get in touch with you in the next few days and let you know where we go from here."

Paul shook the attorney's hand, then Matt's. "We won't keep you waiting long for an answer."

—m—

That night Paul and Anna talked at length about the meeting. They reflected on the conversation and the questions that'd been brought up by each couple. In the end, they decided that the Whitemans' suggestion for what to tell the child about the rape was a good compromise. "I appreciated his apology for not having thought about how it might make you look," Paul told Anna. "And I think there's a lot of wisdom in what Matthew came up with after that."

Anna agreed, and before they crawled into the bed "down the stairs" that night, they decided they would offer the Whitemans the opportunity to adopt Anna's child.

She turned on her side, facing away from Paul—the only comfortable position she could find in her advanced state of pregnancy. Paul put his arms around her, his hands caressing her rounded stomach. They lay in silence that way until they fell asleep.

Nineteen

The shrill ring of the telephone startled Anna as she stood at the sink washing the few dishes that had accumulated through the morning. She hurriedly dried her hands and picked up the receiver.

"Anna?"

"Dad! It's so good to hear your voice." Anna had spoken to her mother earlier in the week, but her father had been out of town then, and Anna had not heard his voice in almost two weeks.

"How are you?" Her father's voice sounded weary and sad.

She knew immediately that something was wrong. "Dad, what is it?"

"Honey, your grandmother died this morning."

Her tears flowed freely as the realization dawned. Grandmother Cavender was gone. A year ago this news would have come as a mild surprise, accompanied by relief that the struggle was over—for both her grandmother and for her mother.

She'd known this phone call could not be many months away, yet now, coming as it did on the heels of everything else, it stunned her.

"Oh, Dad! I'm so sorry? When did it happen?"

"Your mother found her about seven o'clock this morning when she went in to wake her for breakfast. The doctor said she died in her sleep, very peacefully."

Anna couldn't speak for a moment. She swallowed hard. "Is Mom doing okay?"

"Don't you worry…she's handling it just fine. Although your mother would never, ever have called your grandmother a burden, I know it's a relief to her that it's finally over. Aunt Lila is in Montana at Bob and Carla's, so the funeral won't be until Tuesday morning. It'll be at the church, of course."

Anna felt as though she had been struck. *The funeral!* She hadn't thought of that. And she would not be there. She would not be able to say her final goodbyes to the grandmother she had adored, would not be able to offer her mother the comfort of a shoulder to cry on, an arm to lean on. The respect that her presence would have signified would be called into question by all the aunts, uncles, and cousins she loved dearly, and saw so rarely.

"Oh, Dad. What am I going to do about the funeral?"

"You'll do the only thing you can do, honey. You'll think about us and pray for us. You'll cry with us and remember with us. And you'll not feel one ounce of guilt that you are doing it from afar."

Her father knew her so well. Already she was eaten up with guilt. "Oh, Dad. I so want to be there with you. I… What will you tell people? They'll *expect* me to be there."

"Don't you worry about that. We'll do what we have to do. You just take care of yourself and put this out of your mind. You have plenty to deal with, Annie, without taking this on your shoulders too."

She teared up again hearing her father use her childhood nickname.

They talked for a while about Grandmother Cavender. Stella Cavender had been a remarkable woman, full of spunk and wisdom. Anna knew that her joy for life and her legacy of faith would live on in her children and grandchildren.

Her dad stayed on the phone with her for half an hour, allowing her the comfort of remembrance, and when Anna told him goodbye, there was gratitude in her heart, both for the privilege of having known her grandmother and for the blessing God had given her in her father.

Paul called after lunch, and he and Anna debated about whether or not he or the girls would attend the funeral.

"It seems that someone from our family should be there, Anna. But if you're not there with us, we will need an explanation for your absence. I suppose the best thing would be to say that you're not feeling well."

She frowned. "Well, that wouldn't altogether be a lie."

"No, I guess it wouldn't."

"Oh, Paul. I don't know what to say. I feel awful about this. Why did this have to happen just now?"

He sighed. "I've simply quit asking that question, babe. I don't know the answer, and I'm not certain we'll ever know on this earth. Despite it all, somehow I still don't doubt God's goodness."

"No, Paul. I don't either. I *don't* doubt it, but I certainly don't understand it either." She knew that Paul's faith was being tested as greatly as her own. She suspected he spoke the words almost as if to convince himself they were true— that God still *was* good. Anna sometimes marveled that she still believed it. Yet, in a strange way, the fact that she could survive her circumstances and continue to believe in God's goodness confirmed her faith.

She and Paul talked for a while and finally agreed that he would go with Kassi—and Kara if she was willing. They would represent Anna at the funeral, make excuses for her to the relatives, and pray that God would forgive them their minor deceit.

—⟋∿⟍—

Paul called Kara at her apartment that evening. When she recovered from initial tears, she told him, "I know it's a relief for Grandma, though. Grandpa too." She hesitated. "How's Mom taking it?" Ordinarily she avoided mentioning her mother, though Paul always updated her on Anna anyway.

"She's handling it as well as you might expect. Mostly she's upset because she won't be able to be at the funeral. Honey, I really think you girls and I ought to go for Grandma Greyson's sake. I haven't gotten hold of Kassi yet, but I'm sure she'll want to be there. Do you think you could make arrangements to get away?"

Kara was silent for an overlong moment, but finally she said, "Yeah. I'll work something out. Do you want me to call Kassi?"

"Well, I need to talk to her anyway, but if you want to call her to work out transportation, that would be good. I assume you girls will come to Chicago first?"

"Yes. I'd like to ride to the church with you if that's okay."

"Sure," he said. "And listen, I'm not sure how we're going to handle questions about Mom's absence. Grandma and Grandpa and Aunt Liz are the only ones who'll be there that know the real story, so, much as I hate it, we're going to have to...fudge a little. I told Mom we'd just say she wasn't feeling well and leave it at that. It's not altogether untrue..." he trailed off lamely. Paul simply could not bring himself to use the word *lie*, yet he knew that in reality it probably would be a lie that they used to explain why Anna wasn't there. *Lord, forgive us.*

"No, I suppose it's not," Kara said. "How...how is Mom... healthwise?"

"She's doing okay. Everything is going fine with the baby. But, I'm sure you can imagine that this isn't easy for her. I don't want to force the issue—it has to be between you and Mom, and I know you well enough to know that I sure can't change your mind—but it would mean so much to your mom if you could put aside your differences until this is over. I don't think you realize how much it hurts her to be at odds with you—*especially* now. She's already made her decision and that's not going to change now."

He heard his daughter's familiar sigh at the other end and feared he'd said too much. They'd had variations of this conversation half a dozen times in the past months.

"Dad, what am I supposed to say to her? You know how I feel about this whole thing. It didn't have to be this way. Mom didn't *have* to go through this. It could have been so simple. I can't in honesty tell her anything different."

He struggled to keep the anger from his voice. "Kara, I'm not asking you to change your opinion. I'm simply asking you to accept the fact that Mom—and I—made a choice. *We're* living with it, and we're the ones who will suffer whatever consequences come of it."

"Then why am I going to a funeral where I'll be forced to lie through my teeth about my mother's absence?"

Though her words started out dripping with sarcasm, Paul could hear in her voice that she immediately regretted it. "I'm sorry, Dad. That wasn't fair. I know you don't really have much choice. But do you see what I mean?"

She did have a point about their deceit, and it stung him to realize it. Yet he felt helpless to do anything different. They certainly couldn't give away Anna's circumstances. That wouldn't be right either. It seemed an impossible predicament.

"Kara, you're right," he said finally. "It was inevitable that our decision would in some way affect you. But surely you can appreciate the moral consideration—the *conviction*— that impelled us to decide the way we did. Surely you can see that," he repeated, growing frustrated.

"Dad, you can't imagine how much I have thought about

this ever since you and Mom told us what happened."

For the first time since it all began, Paul heard uncertainty, contrition maybe, in her voice, and he sent up a prayer that his daughter's heart was softening.

"I'll just tell you, Dad," Kara continued, "I'm kind of confused right now. You surely know that I haven't turned ultra pro-abortion or anything like that. But I do think there are times when it is the lesser of two evils. And if *ever* there was an instance where that is true, it's Mom's situation. She thinks she's doing some heroic thing saving this baby's life, but she's destroying a lot of other lives in the process."

"I think that's a bit extreme, Kara. I don't think anyone's life is being *destroyed*. Inconvenienced, yes, but only for a time. Surely a child's life is worth nine months of inconvenience."

"And what kind of life is that child going to have?"

Paul had heard her argument before. Kara was growing emotional, and Paul didn't want to argue with her over the phone. "Let's not get into it right now. We'll talk some more on the drive Tuesday, if you want, okay? And I'm sorry if I'm nagging you. It's just that I can't stand to see the silence between you and your mom. I love you, honey. And she loves you more than you can possibly know."

"I love you too, Dad. Tell Mom...tell her I'm thinking about her."

"That will mean a lot to her, honey. Thank you."

—⚏—

The morning of the funeral Paul got up early to get the house straightened for the girls' arrival. He made the bed and put his breakfast dishes in the dishwasher before heading for the shower.

How he dreaded this day. He fully expected to have it out with Kara on the ride to the funeral. And he certainly wasn't looking forward to facing Anna's relatives, trying to explain her absence. He had racked his brain and pleaded with the Lord for some other explanation that would be more truthful, but there simply wasn't any. He'd never been a liar, and he wasn't sure he could even pull this deception off.

When he emerged from the shower, the telephone was ringing. He wrapped a towel around his waist and raced down the hall to their bedroom.

"Hello."

"Paul? I was beginning to think you'd left already." It was Anna.

"Hi, sweetheart. No. The girls won't be here until about nine. I was in the shower."

"Oh, I'm sorry."

"It's okay. I was just drying off. So how are you this morning?"

"I…I'm sicker than a dog, Paul."

"What do you mean?"

"I don't know. I must have caught a flu bug or something. I woke up about four this morning feeling just miserable, and I'm not a whole lot better right now."

"Do you think you need to see a doctor?" He was alarmed. She sounded awful.

"No…no, probably not. I'm not running a fever. I'm just terribly sick to my stomach, and I can't seem to keep anything down. Maybe it was something I ate."

"Oh, babe, I'm so sorry. I wish I could be there with you."

"Believe me, it would not be pleasant."

"Is there somebody you can call to take you to the doctor if you get worse? Is Tanya there?"

"Yes. She called this morning to see if I wanted to have lunch with her. But"—she groaned—"Lunch? I don't even want to think about it. Anyway, Tanya said she'll be home all day, so don't worry about me. I'm sure I'll be fine, but I sure feel miserable right now."

"I'm sorry. We'll be praying for you."

"Thank, babe." Anna paused and then a smile came into

her voice. "You know what I think, Paul?"

"No. What?"

"I think—this might sound crazy—but do you think maybe this is God's way of giving me an excuse for not being at Grandmother's funeral?"

"Oh, wow... I didn't even think about that." He chuckled. "I'm so sorry you're so sick, but you have no idea how happy this makes me. I can hardly wait to tell all your relatives how miserably sick you are!"

"Well, thanks a lot," she said. But her weak laughter told him she understood perfectly.

They marveled at the perfect timing of this flu bug, and Anna giggled with him about it—until she had to say a hurried goodbye and rush to the bathroom.

Paul hung up laughing, reflecting that the Lord certainly did "move in mysterious ways, His wonders to perform."

Twenty

Winter's first snow had fallen the night before, and the streets of Chicago looked like a Christmas wonderland. Thanksgiving had come and gone, and people were just beginning to put up their Christmas lights and hang wreaths on their doors.

The Marquette house on Fairmont Avenue remained unadorned, however. The decorating had always been Anna's department. Paul didn't even know where she stored the boxes of ornaments and lights. Besides, she would be home before Christmas. The doctor in Fort Wayne seemed to think the baby could come earlier than Anna's December 13 due date.

And having her home was all he could think about. Thanksgiving had been incredibly lonely. The ad agency had taken on a new large account, and he'd had no choice but to work Friday after the holiday, which meant he couldn't be with Anna. He and the girls had gone to his mom's in the morning, then had a late lunch with Jack and Charlotte. It was good to be with people who knew the terrible secret of his life—good to not have to put on a front like he did everywhere else. But he couldn't enjoy the holiday, knowing how desperately homesick and sad—*and alone*—Anna must be feeling.

Still, his time with his daughters had been special. Kara truly did seem to have softened a bit. Though she'd never taken her anger at Anna out on him, he thought he detected a kinder tone in her voice when Anna's name was mentioned.

Kara and Kassi had cooked for him and helped with the housework, though there wasn't much to be done with Shirley coming in each week to look after Paul and the house.

Kara had even offered to help Paul put up the Christmas decorations. He'd hated to decline her offer. Her thoughtfulness seemed such a positive sign. But he couldn't bear to have the house looking festive and cheerful when Anna wasn't there to make it truly so. He was grateful she would be home in time for Christmas. It wouldn't be a happy Christmas. It would be a time of grieving and healing, but Paul would be joyful just to have her back in their home. And he looked forward to a quiet celebration of her homecoming.

He'd just buttoned his heavy winter coat, gathered up his briefcase and gym bag, and opened the back door to leave for work when the phone rang. Sighing heavily, he tossed everything into a pile on the kitchen table and hurried to pick up the handset before the answering machine came on.

"Hello?"

"Paul Marquette, please."

"This is he."

"Mr. Marquette, this is Joseph Holden, Orlando Police Department."

Paul's heart began to race. Instantly, his thoughts were carried back to that awful week in Florida. "Yes?" Paul answered.

"I'm calling with good news, Mr. Marquette. The man who attacked your wife was arrested this morning." He went on to tell Paul that a man had been brought in for questioning after attacking a woman. After hearing the testimony of witnesses to that attempted rape, several officers had recalled the similarities to Anna's case and others that had happened in the area. They'd pulled her files and compared notes.

"You won't believe this, Mr. Marquette," Officer Holden said. "It was the cologne thing that tipped us off."

After the incident when Anna and the girls had gone shopping at the mall in Fort Wayne, Paul had called Orlando to report Anna's recollection of the cologne the rapist had possibly been wearing. The officers Paul had spoken with seemed to feel the information was insignificant. He'd tended to agree with them, but nevertheless, he'd felt obligated to report it. And in the back of his mind, he'd hoped perhaps it *would* prove to be the final piece of the puzzle that would put this beast behind bars where he belonged.

Now the officer explained what had happened. "Our man struck again just last week, same place where your wife was attacked—there at Longwood. A couple of college kids came upon the scene, and they fought the guy off before he hurt the girl too badly. They held him down while she ran for help. He hasn't exactly confessed anything yet, but this young lady stayed pretty calm. She identified him, and he fits the brief description you gave us in the hospital. Funny thing was, since this guy was black, none of that really clicked until this gal mentioned the smell of that cologne. But then I got to thinking— French accent, six and a half feet tall, the Longwood location. Something clicked, and I remembered your call."

Paul was writing as fast as his fingers could put the letters down. He knew in his excitement he was likely to forget half of what the man was saying. Now, one word stared back at him from the notepad on which he had been scribbling: BLACK. The man was black? There must be some mistake. This couldn't be the right man. Anna's attacker had been French. Anna had been sure his accent was French.

She would have recognized it, having studied French in high school and college. In fact, that was one of the few things she *had* been certain about. Paul fought to concentrate on what the policeman was saying—something about them wanting Anna to come to Orlando. To identify the man? To testify against him? He'd lost track of the conversation, but he had to know. "Did you say this suspect is black?"

"That's right. He's French, like your wife thought. French-African—and over here illegally. He's probably wanted on all kinds of warrants back in France. We're still checking into that…"

The officer's voice droned on, but Paul no longer heard his words. He was still trying to grasp what this news meant for them. For Anna. If it was true—if the man they'd arrested really was the man who raped Anna—then the child she was carrying, the child she was soon to give birth to, would be biracial. And probably dark skinned.

Stunned, struggling to absorb what the officer was saying, he managed to explain that Anna would not be able to travel anytime soon. He mentioned her pregnancy without telling the man just how irrevocably her pregnancy was tied to the news the officer had just delivered.

Officer Holden promised to keep them posted on any new developments. "Meanwhile," he said, "you can rest assured the man is behind bars and won't be out anytime this century if I have anything to say about it."

Paul hung up and sat staring at the phone for a long time, not sure what to do next. It was only Tuesday. On Friday he'd planned to go to New Haven and stay until the baby was born, but he was swamped at the office. For weeks now, he'd been leaving early on Fridays to make the trip to see Anna. The lost hours had left his desk piled with work, and now he simply had to get things in order before he took the three weeks of vacation he'd requested.

Since John Vickers was the only one at Lindell & Bachman who knew his situation, there would be little sympathy for a request for yet more time off. Paul saw no way that he could be with Anna before Friday.

Then it dawned on him that the Whitemans, too, deserved—no, *needed*—to know this new information. What would the young couple's reaction be when they heard? It could change everything they'd agreed upon. Still, they had to be told immediately.

Thoughts raced through his mind more swiftly than he could process them. He thought of the Whitemans' excitement when they'd learned they would finally be parents. But would it even be right now, knowing what he knew, to give this baby to a white couple? What was best for a child of mixed race? It was a question he'd never pondered. Never had to. Had the contract they signed locked them into an irrevocable arrangement?

Paul was desperate to talk to Anna. Yet, he'd collected his wits enough to realize that this news would be staggering to Anna. It was simply not something he could tell her over the telephone. Not just that the rapist had been identified, but that his identity might change all the decisions they'd made to this point.

Anna's emotions had been fragile recently. She'd always been affected that way during the final months of her pregnancies. And of course, this pregnancy had its own unique set of complications. But how could he talk to her on the phone each day until Friday and pretend nothing had changed?

But wait… Emma had gone to New Haven for the week. She'd called him before she left Friday night, as she nearly always did before she went to visit her daughter, generously offering to stop by his house and pick up anything he might want to send along to Anna.

Paul composed himself and dialed Emma's cell phone, praying that she and Anna weren't together.

Emma answered on the first ring.

"Paul. Hello. How are you?" The warmth in Emma's voice reminded him that she would help Anna through this.

"Hi, Emma. Anna doesn't happen to be with you, does she?"

"No. I haven't seen her yet this morning, but I thought I heard the television downstairs a few minutes ago. She's not answering her phone?"

"I didn't try calling. I've just had some...news." He'd been so close to saying *bad* news. But for him to call this bad news would be insensitive, would likely seem insulting to Emma. He truly wasn't thinking of the news as bad because it meant the child would be of mixed race. But it was bad news in that it complicated things and created a whole new realm of questions about what was best for the baby. And he knew it would be terribly upsetting for Anna.

She'd worried incessantly that her child would face feelings of rejection because of being adopted and because of the birth father's crime. Now she would have the added worry about issues of race that would certainly affect the child.

But Emma would understand all that. Even the fact that they'd almost certainly caught her rapist would cause Anna great consternation. She'd tried desperately to put the rape out of her mind, had accepted that they would never find the rapist, and therefore, she would never have to face him. Paul knew Anna took great comfort in that supposition.

Now he tried to organize his thoughts as he revealed to Emma what he'd discovered. "Here's what's going on. I received a call from Orlando a few minutes ago. They are fairly certain that they have found Anna's rapist."

"Oh, my. That's good news... I guess."

"It is, yes. But of course it's going to be upsetting to Anna. I think she's hoped she'd never have to hear of him again. But, Emma, there's more." He paused, clearing his throat. "The man they arrested is French-African—that's why Anna noticed the accent. But...he's black. Of course, you realize this means that the baby she's carrying is biracial."

"Oh Paul," Emma breathed into the phone. "What can I do?"

Relieved to hear only compassion in her voice, he said, "It's absolutely unfair to put this on you, but is there any way you could be with Anna when I call her tonight? She'll need someone, and I know you'll be able to comfort her, to…help her process all this. I simply can't get away from the office before Friday, but neither can I keep this news from her."

"Of course, Paul. Of course, I'll be there."

They agreed on a time for Paul to call, and Emma assured him she would be right beside Anna when he told her.

—ш—

Anna was lying on the sofa trying to get comfortable when she heard Emma's familiar knock on the door to the basement apartment. A Christmas special was on the television, but the volume was turned so low it was barely audible. She'd had trouble summoning the Christmas spirit, but the sounds from the TV set helped ease her loneliness somewhat.

Before she could answer the knock, Emma called out her name. "Anna?"

"Come on in. It's not locked."

Emma opened the door and stuck her head around. Seeing Anna in a reclining position, she hurriedly motioned for Anna to stay put. "Don't get up. I was just wondering how you were feeling."

Anna sat up and patted the couch beside her. "Sit down. I'm feeling fat—that's how I'm feeling." She sighed, and in a sing-song voice she recited the pitiful litany that had been running through her head all day. "I can't lie on my side without the baby kicking me. I can't lie on my back because it hurts too much. For obvious reasons I can't lie on my stomach…" She looked down at the object of her discomfort, and they both laughed.

"You really are getting *huge*, girl. How much longer do you have to go?" Emma teased.

"I predict this child will weigh in at ten pounds. At least

I hope so. I'm beginning to wonder if I'll ever get my figure back. Not that it was anything to brag about before, but—"

Her cell phone interrupted her. Anna saw Emma's smile dim and her eyes darken as she stared at the phone. Did Emma know something she didn't?

Anna looked at the caller ID. It was Paul. "I'd better take this," she told Emma.

Instead of excusing herself, Emma sat down beside her.

Something was going on. Trying to read Emma's expression, she answered Paul. "Hi, honey. What's up?"

"Hi, babe. How are you feeling?"

"I'm fine…"

"Good. Is Emma there with you?"

"Yes …" Something was wrong. She could hear it in his voice. "What's wrong, Paul? Something's happened, hasn't it?"

"Yes, Anna."

She struggled for breath. "Are the girls okay?"

"Yes. Yes, the girls are fine. It's…nothing like that. But…I had a call from Orlando today."

As she listened to Paul's gentle voice, Emma reached out and took her hand. Anna saw that she was watching her face intently. Whatever it was, Emma already knew what was coming.

"Anna," he said, speaking slowly and precisely. "They found the man who raped you."

She listened in shocked silence as Paul explained about the phone call he'd received earlier today.

She felt an odd hysteria rising up inside her as the implication of his words soaked in. She squeezed Emma's hand. "Paul, what… what are you telling me? What are you saying?"

"Anna… Honey, please calm down."

"Do you mean… ?" She couldn't finish the sentence. She felt drained. As the truth of his news sank in, she felt every ounce of strength seep out of her body. She crumpled against Emma's strong body and sobbed. How much more did God expect them to take?

She had carried a picture of this child in her mind—a little blond replica of Kara and Kassi when they'd been small. Except, for some reason she'd always felt she was carrying a boy. More than once, it had crossed her mind that this might turn out to be the son they'd never had. And she pictured a little Kevin, the name she and Paul had always wanted to use for a boy.

At times it had been hard not to think of this baby as her own. At first, after she'd finally accepted that she was truly pregnant, she'd had to continually remind herself that she would be giving this child up, that it would not be her singing lullabies and reading fairy tales in the rocking chair. She realized that it would be difficult to give those things up, because those were the things that would redeem the circumstances of this birth. Those were the things that would heal this child who'd been sired by a criminal, rejected by his own mother, given away to be adopted by strangers. Anna had so many fears for this baby, fears for too many things that would be *her* fault.

After they'd met the Whitemans—after that decision had been made she'd worked through her feelings, putting some of those fears to rest. She'd pictured the same little blond boy being loved and cared for by Matt and Jeanine. He would look in the mirror and see that he looked much like his mother. Or his father. Sometimes Anna wondered if she'd chosen the Whitemans in part because they *looked* like they could be the parents of the baby she imagined. They would protect him from the awful truth of his past. They would become the branches on his family tree, and when the time came, they would soften the blow of *her* rejection. When the baby was older, the Whitemans would make excuses for a father who didn't know the ramifications of his sin. She'd truly been comforted by that picture.

Now she was being told that her child would probably carry with him every day—in the very color of his skin—the burden of being different from his parents. Of wondering why his friends all looked like their mother or their father, and he so obviously did not really belong with the people he called "Mommy and Daddy." Could a child survive the double blow of such differences—not only being adopted and having a horrible secret about his past, but of having his very appearance cry out the news to the whole world?

Anna remembered her own daughters making family trees in second grade, and she wondered how this little one would fill in the branches, how he would answer his teachers when they asked him from which country his ancestors had come. And when strangers in the grocery store asked the Whitemans, "And whose side of the family does he look like?" how would they reply? In truth, that question would now probably be left unspoken, wondered silently with curious sideways glances.

But the child wouldn't miss those stares. And as he grew, he would understand their meaning only too well.

Anna sobbed into the phone, "Oh, Paul, my baby...my poor baby. He doesn't have a chance. How will he ever overcome everything he'll be starting out with? How?" Her voice turned angry. "I can't take this. Not another thing! Do you hear me?" She knew it wasn't fair to spew her anger on Paul.

But he let her cry, let her rail and shake her fists. Her keening filled the room, a low wailing sound that frightened her, because she had no control over it.

Emma put an arm around her and patted her shoulder, and across the miles, her sweet husband murmured words of love.

Finally, spent, Anna handed the phone to Emma and sank back into the cushions of the sofa, her voice stilled, her eyes burning.

"I'll be here, Paul," Emma reassured him. "I'll stay here all night if I need to."

Anna heard him thank her, heard the anguish in his voice and knew that it was killing him not to be able to take her into his arms and comfort her through this storm.

For the next hour, Emma sat beside her, held her hand, cried with her. Finally, she found her words. They were rational, reasonable questions, asked of necessity.

"What does it do to a child, Emma, to grow up with dark skin in a white family? Do you think this child could survive that kind of identity crisis on top of the whole adoption question? Would he ever feel like he belongs anywhere? Would I be deserting him... if I give him up? Am I taking away the only chance he has to truly belong somewhere? I've never thought much about racial issues. It's...it's never been directed at me, so I've never had to face it."

Emma had told Anna once that she'd faced more prejudice as a single mother than she had as a black woman. But she'd also confided that Daniel and Tanya *had* faced opposition when they'd first moved into their mostly white neighborhood in New Haven. They were one of only a few black families in the small town, and though they were accepted and even embraced by the little community now, it had taken time. Anna knew, also, that Tanya and Daniel worried that as Justin grew older and entered school, he would invariably face questions about the dark skin that singled him out. It was so wrong, yet it seemed to be a sad truth of human nature.

How would the Whitemans, Matthew and Jeanine, face the bigotry they were almost sure to come up against simply because their child was of a different race?

Would Matt and Jeanine still want her baby? She voiced the frightening thought to Emma.

Emma reached out and turned Anna's tear-stained face toward her, forcing her to look into her dark, piercing eyes. "Anna," she said fiercely, "even if the Whitemans do change their mind, somebody will want your baby. Somebody *will* love him, and care for him, and cry with him, and laugh with him." She spoke the thought like a poem, and Anna took comfort in the beauty of her friend's words.

Because of the Rain

Twenty-one

Paul phoned Walter LeMans the following morning. He explained the new development to the attorney, who listened with concern.

"Do you have any opinions on what would be best for a child of mixed race?" Paul asked the lawyer. "We want what is best for the baby, but I admit this has thrown us for a loop."

"I can certainly understand why," LeMans said.

Paul sighed. "Anna already worries that the child might suffer because of his background—being a child of rape, being adopted. Anna sees it as her rejection of him. And then add this to the mix and… I wonder if there are any studies that would point us one direction or another. Would it be in the child's best interest to be raised in a black family? One where he will most likely resemble his adoptive parents? Or does that really matter?"

LeMans rubbed his smooth-shaven chin. "I'm not aware of any studies that offer proof of one line of thinking over another. I do know that there are some in the African-American community who believe strongly that black children should be placed in African-American families. Of course, that isn't always possible, and personally, I feel there are other factors that are more important than the race issue. Surely the stability of the marriage, and the love and commitment a family can offer a child make a greater difference than the racial issue." His tone became thoughtful. "I wish I could offer you a more definitive answer, Paul, but I don't have one. I guess the first thing we need to do is visit with the Whitemans and see how they feel about it. I'm sorry this has been so difficult, and I certainly understand your concerns. I'll do some checking and see if I can find some information that will be helpful."

"Thank you. I'll hop online and do my own research tonight, too."

LeMans assured Paul that he would inform the Whitemans and secure a definite answer from them by the end of the week.

When Paul got home from work later that night, the message light was flashing on the answering machine. He pushed the playback button.

Walter LeMans' rich voice filled the room. "Paul, it's five-thirty, Wednesday afternoon. I was hoping to catch you at home. I've spoken with the Whitemans, and they would like to meet with you as soon as possible. I would appreciate it if you could give me a call at your earliest convenience. Feel free to call me at home." The attorney went on to leave his home number and ended the message with, "Please call me as soon as possible." Paul detected a note of urgency in his voice.

He checked his watch and dialed the number.

"Thank you for getting back to me so quickly," LeMans said when he came on the line. "I'm afraid I have some disturbing news."

Paul waited in silence for the inevitable announcement.

"The Whitemans want to explain their reasons to you in person, but the long and short of it is they do not feel they can take the baby under the present circumstances."

Paul shook his head. "I was afraid that might happen." He sighed deeply. "I'm not sure Anna can take another blow like this."

"I understand. I'm so sorry, Paul, but under the circumstances, I think the Whitemans made the right decision. They'll explain everything when we get together. Will you be coming to Indiana this weekend?"

"Yes. In fact, I'm coming down Friday to stay until the baby is born. But I have to wrap things up at the agency here before I leave, so it will be impossible for me to get there before late Friday afternoon. Would a four o'clock Friday appointment work for you and the Whitemans?"

"I'll make it work. We should also probably go over some more resumés while we're together. I know Anna is very near delivery, and I would hate for the baby to have to go into foster care before we can arrange an adoption."

Paul hadn't thought of that. But agreed with him. He hung up the phone, a myriad of questions churning in his mind. He knew Anna must be having the same questions. It was too late to call her now, as she'd been going to bed earlier in this last month of her pregnancy. He wondered how she was taking things.

Still, he trusted Emma to say the right words. Anna was in good hands with her, but he also knew that her emotions were frayed beyond the breaking point. And the baby was due in less than two weeks.

—❦—

It was a solemn group that sat around Walter LeMans' desk Friday afternoon. Jeanine Whiteman's red eyes looked like Anna was sure her own did. How many tears had been shed over this child?

Paul looked utterly exhausted, and Matthew Whiteman's expression mirrored Paul's. She worried about her husband

and all he'd had to bear up under these last nine months.

After a rather formal statement of the reason for the meeting, Walter LeMans turned to the Whitemans. "I appreciate your willingness to speak with the Marquettes in person. I know this is difficult for you, and I'm sure they appreciate that as well." He nodded in Matthew's direction.

Looking nervous and unsure of himself, the young man cleared his throat. Beside him, Jeanine dabbed at her eyes and pressed her lips tightly together.

"We are very sorry," Matt began. "There is nothing we would like more than to take your baby and raise him and love him. But...well, if there is any chance that this baby would be of another race...or biracial...my father would never accept a child like that...a child that was not white." He hung his head, shame apparent in his countenance. With obvious effort he continued. "That was one reason we didn't want to tell anyone about how the baby was conceived. My father...he—I love my father," Matt finally blurted, "but he is a very opinionated, prejudiced man, and it wouldn't be fair to put a child through the kind of rejection I fear my father is capable of. We...we would have loved your baby with all our hearts." He broke down then, and his wife reached for his hand as he slumped into the chair and buried his head in his hands.

Paul put a hand on the young man's shoulder. "I'm sorry for you, Matthew, I truly am. We felt very positive about giving the baby to you and Jeanine. But I believe you have done the right thing. You've done what's best for this baby. We'll pray that the Lord will bless you with another chance to be parents."

Anna wanted to add her own approval to what Paul had told them. She believed they truly did have the child's best interests at heart, and she admired their courage in letting their dream go, in making this sacrifice for a child they already loved as their own. She could imagine how devastated Jeanine must be feeling now, how tempted she must be to feel hatred toward her father-in-law.

But as much as she wanted to be able to give the Whitemans some expression of comfort, she could not form the words. With great effort she forced a wan smile and nodded in their direction, but already her mind was racing. *What will we do? Where do we turn now that this has fallen through?*

Matthew and Jeanine rose and left the room, heads down. Walter LeMans shook Paul's hand and again offered apologies. Anna watched all this through a haze as she and Paul stood and walked toward the door. She had never felt so near despair. She simply could not think clearheadedly anymore.

One of the mild Braxton Hicks contractions she'd been feeling off and on for the past week began its slow ascent.

"You okay, babe?" Paul's forehead furrowed.

She closed her eyes and bit her lip, leaning heavily against him. After a minute the pain crested and abated. "I'm fine."

They walked down the empty hallway and through the wide doors that opened onto the parking lot. Paul made polite conversation with the lawyer, who had walked them to the door. Anna was silent, unable even to find simple words of farewell.

—◊—

They drove back to the apartment in silence. Paul helped Anna change clothes and tucked her into bed as though she were a small child. Then he went back to the car to carry in two-weeks' worth of luggage.

Anna was asleep by the time he finished unloading the car, and he plopped down, fully clothed, on top of the blankets beside her, too exhausted to unpack his bags. He clasped his hands behind his head and stared, unseeing, at the ceiling.

He must have drifted off because when he opened his eyes next, morning sunlight was streaming through the windows. He'd slept through the night, too exhausted to unpack his bags, or do more than slip his shoes off before lying beside Anna. He eased his legs over the side of the bed and headed for the shower.

Anna was stirring when he emerged from the bathroom twenty minutes later. "Did you sleep okay?"

"Once I finally settled down." She stretched and yawned. "You?"

"I must have. I slept in my clothes."

"I saw that. I didn't want to wake you."

He leaned over the bed and kissed her. "Sleep in if you want. I'll go put the coffee on."

"No, I'm awake."

Paul fixed them a light breakfast of toast, orange juice, and coffee, and they sat companionably in the kitchen, voicing only mundane comments about the food and the weather.

Pouring Anna a forbidden second cup of caffeinated coffee, Paul took a deep breath. "Honey, I think we should go over the other resumés as soon as you feel up to it. LeMans mentioned that if we haven't found a home for the baby by the time it's born, the child would likely go into temporary foster care. I'm sure you'd rather that not be the case..." He let his voice trail off, waiting for her reaction.

"Paul." Anna looked him directly in the eye, and he knew by the set of her jaw and the look in her eyes that what she was about to say had been mulled over through the night and was now spoken with conviction. "I think we should keep this baby...and raise him ourselves."

Paul was stunned. And almost ashamed to admit how relieved he'd been when Anna had told him early in her pregnancy that she wanted to give the baby up for adoption. While he felt it was the best answer for the baby's sake, he admitted with no small measure of guilt that his reasons were less than altruistic. Aside from the selfishness of wanting Anna to himself in their later years, of wanting to be free to travel and free to come and go as they pleased, free even from the financial responsibilities of another child—aside from all that, it terrified him to think of setting out anew on the journey of parenthood at the age of forty-eight. He was healthy and active now—felt no different than he had at thirty-eight. But how many sixty-five-year-old men were capable of supporting a child to adulthood—financially *or* emotionally? He could scarcely imagine having a toddler in the house again. Would he even live long enough to see this child grow up?

As these thoughts raced through his mind, Anna stared into the distance, as she spoke. "It *is* my baby, and it seems that I'm the only one who can protect him. The only one who really loves him. If I let him go, he won't belong to anyone. Shouldn't he have at least one person in this world…one person in his life to whom he truly belongs?"

She looked at Paul with pleading in her eyes, in her voice. "Don't we all deserve to belong somewhere? I can't just desert my baby now. What happened wasn't *his* fault. He shouldn't have to suffer—but he will anyway. He will, and I… I want to be the one to dry his tears and…and tell him how much God loves him…how much *I* love him…" She started to cry.

Paul pushed back his chair and went around the table to her. Helping her from her chair, he put his arms around her, hugging her from behind. They stood that way for a long time, her swollen belly making their embrace awkward and probably uncomfortable for Anna.

He didn't know what to say or how to respond. He'd promised Anna on a long-ago night that he would raise this child and love it as his own, if that was what she wanted. Could he make that promise all over again and mean it?

He searched his heart now. *What had changed?* Was he hesitating now because the baby was biracial? Was there racism in him that he wasn't even aware of?

He searched his heart. And concluded that no, he was not a prejudiced man. Had Anna reckoned, though, that the disclosure of the baby's paternity would make it impossible for Paul to pass himself off as the child's father? Not just to the child, but to anyone else. What would damage the child more—a haunting secret about his past, hinted at with every curious stranger's glance? Or the devastating truth that the father whose genes he carried was a criminal, that his conception had been a tragic event that had physically brutalized and emotionally traumatized his mother?

And too, there were immediate concerns. Anna had been virtually in hiding for nearly three months. If they were to decide to keep this child, they would have to reveal the truth to their extended families, to their church, to the people he worked with, and to Anna's friends at school. The intimate private details of their tragedy would become public knowledge.

It would be extremely difficult. He wasn't sure Anna had thought about all these things.

Then there was Kara. He feared a sudden life-altering decision like this would be another blow to Kara's relationship with her mother.

All these things tumbled through his mind, troubling him greatly. But he said nothing. There were no easy answers. And Anna was exhausted.

Finally, as he had said many months before this nightmare began, Paul repeated, "We'll do what's right, Anna. I don't know what else to say right now. We'll do what's right."

—⁂—

At five o'clock in the morning on December 11, Anna woke with a start. The apartment was quiet, and Paul snored softly beside her in the bed. He he'd been here for ten days now, waiting with her and seeking answers to the impasse they found themselves up against. Despite the dilemma they wrestled with, despite the unsettled decisions, in many ways Anna felt like she was home. Having Paul in her bed again, at her side every day, and knowing that when he went home this time she would go with him was a comfort beyond words.

She placed her hand gently on his back now, absorbing the warmth of his skin, the rhythms of his breathing. Not sure what had awakened her so abruptly, she sat up and eased her legs over the side of the bed. She stretched to work the stiffness out of her joints and padded barefoot into the living room. Nothing seemed amiss, but now she was fully awake. She made a trip to the bathroom and, not wanting to wake Paul, came back out to the living room and stretched out on the sofa.

She hadn't been there ten minutes when she was gripped by a strong contraction. The Braxton Hicks contractions, normal during late pregnancy, had come and gone with some regularity in the past few weeks, but there was no mistaking this crescendo of pain. As the minutes passed, Anna grew certain she was in labor.

Though she'd waited through the interminable weeks and months that'd led to this day, though she'd longed to have this day over with, she suddenly could hardly fathom that it had at last arrived.

She held out a hand and realized she was trembling. Fear rose in her throat for the pain and hard work of labor that lay ahead of her, for the encounter that would bring her face-to-face with the baby—*her* baby—whom she had grown to love fiercely.

Whispering a prayer, she padded into the bedroom to awaken Paul.

—⁓—

"Push, Anna, push." The doctor's voice seemed inordinately loud in Anna's ears. For nearly twelve hours she had labored to bring forth a baby who seemed reluctant to make an entrance into the world. Though the pain was not yet excruciating, her exhaustion was. She wasn't sure she could push even one more time.

Steeling herself for the wave of pain due to wash over

her any second, Anna tightened her grip on Paul's hands. He stood behind her at the head of the labor bed, wiping her forehead with a cool cloth, letting her grip his hands during each contraction, and whispering intimate words of love and encouragement in her ear.

As the next contraction began its ascent, she felt her body take over as though it performed apart from her mind or strength. With an intensity that came from some unknown reservoir, she pushed, straining until her lungs were emptied. She gasped for air and another contraction seized her, rolling over her with fury. An involuntary cry, guttural and primitive, escaped her throat.

"You're doing great, Anna," the doctor called from his stool at the foot of the labor bed. "One more time. I can see the baby's head. Come on now. One more time. Push."

Paul took Anna's head in his hands, smoothed the palms of his hands over her forehead and cheeks. "You're doing great, babe. You're doing just great. It's almost over..." His voice broke, and with the back of his hand he swiped at a tear rolling down his cheek.

As the contraction reached its apex, Anna felt the baby slide from her body. With immense relief, she let her body relax. It was over.

Anxiously, she looked down at the doctor and nurses whose attention had shifted away from her. They worked methodically, silently, as one. And then, timeless miracle that it was and always would be, the baby took its first ragged breath and released it in a lusty cry. Was there ever a sweeter sound?

"It's a girl, Anna. A big, healthy girl."

A girl! Anna had imagined this moment again and again in the past months. Imagined it with dread, afraid that she would break down, that it would be unbearable. But now she felt a wan smile tug at the corners of her mouth. And joy took her unawares.

Two nurses had taken the baby to a table on the other side of the room, and Anna turned her head, watching them wash and dress the infant while the doctor attended to her, delivering the placenta and beginning to stitch her up.

"My goodness!" Anna heard a nurse exclaim. "This baby weighs almost ten pounds—exactly nine-fourteen! And twenty inches long."

They brought the baby to her then and placed her—still damp and new—in Anna's arms. The baby was wrapped in a thin flannel blanket, but tiny hands worked themselves loose and waved almost frantically in the air. With reverence, Anna looked into eyes squinted tightly shut against the room's bright lights. She touched soft corkscrew curls that lay wet and fragrant on the rounded scalp. Cherub lips worked themselves into a round O, already rooting against Anna's arm.

The black frizz of hair and the shape of the baby's features left no doubt as to her ancestry. Anna knew that what they'd suspected was true. But as she held her child—her *daughter...oh, another daughter!*—she marveled at her sweetness. The infant was perfect. Healthy and beautiful and perfect.

Anna was filled with love for her. Overwhelmed. And then a realization spread through her being. Just as this new life was pushed from her body, Anna's fear and pain had been pushed away as well. The details of the baby's conception began to fade like shadows in the sunlight. In an ironic, yet miraculous way, this baby's birth had completed her healing.

She smiled up at Paul. She could see by the look of confusion on his face that he didn't grasp her joy. But he gave her a feeble smile and stroked damp hair away from her face with a tenderness that moved her deeply.

Paul moved to her side and looked down at the baby. He reached out tentatively and let the tiny hand rest in his large palm. The contrast brought a lump to Anna's throat.

"Oh, babe. She's beautiful. *You're* beautiful." He squeezed Anna's shoulder with his other hand.

Anna reached up and touched her own hair, damp and stringy, her face, devoid of makeup. She knew she looked far from beautiful right now, but she *felt* it.

For long minutes she held the baby and they marveled at each tiny feature. Her fingers and toes were long and slender. Her forehead and the bridge of her nose were broad, and her eyes—when she finally opened them—were dark and bright and already seemed full of curiosity.

Anna cuddled the little girl in her arms and consciously put every other thought out of her mind, allowing only the joy of the moment to hold her attention. She felt herself grow deliciously drowsy. She was afraid she would fall asleep while the baby still lay in her arms, so Paul summoned the nurses for her. One took the baby to the hospital's nursery while another settled Anna in a small private room down the hall.

Paul kissed Anna goodbye and went home to call their families with the bittersweet news.

In the sterile quietness of her room, Anna closed her eyes and relished the warmth of the blankets the nurses had piled on her. Especially she savored the feeling of weightlessness. After months of carrying a growing baby inside her body—a big baby—now she felt as though she were floating in the bed.

She turned her head and fixed her gaze on the empty bassinet at the side of her bed, and she relived the events of the last few hours over and over. Finally, exhausted, she allowed slumber to overtake her.

—◊◊—

"Mrs. Marquette... Mrs. Marquette?"

Anna heard her name as thought it were coming through a tunnel. She struggled to open her eyes. A nurse stood over her, waiting for a reply. Anna came fully awake, remembering where she was. And it all came rushing back to her. Her baby—her *daughter*—had been born today!

"What time is it?" she croaked.

"It's almost eleven o'clock."

The drapes were drawn, and she felt disoriented. Was it

morning or nighttime?

"I'm sorry to wake you so late," the nurse said, answering Anna's unspoken question, "but your baby is awake and crying. We weren't sure if you wanted us to bring her in or not." Obviously the nursing staff had been made aware of Anna's unique situation.

"Would you like me to bring her to you?" the nurse repeated.

"Yes," Anna said, her voice a whisper. "Yes."

A few minutes later the same nurse backed into the room, opening the door with a shove of her ample hips. In her arms was a tightly swaddled bundle, now still and quiet.

"Wouldn't you know it. By the time I got back to the nursery, she'd calmed down." She shifted the baby to one arm, carrying her in a football hold, obviously very accustomed to working with newborns. With her free hand she helped Anna find the remote and put the bed in an upright position. Then she bent down and put the baby in Anna's arms.

"They tried to give her a little bit of formula in the nursery, but she didn't seem very interested." The nurse handed Anna a warm bottle of formula. "I'll come back in a few minutes and check on you. Here's your call button. Just buzz if you need anything."

"Thank you," Anna said distractedly.

The nurse hurried from the room, and Anna turned her full attention to the bundle in her arms.

The tiny girl's eyes were open, and they immediately focused on Anna's face. Love welled up so strongly in her heart it was almost a physical sensation. She remembered feeling exactly this way when she'd held Kara and Kassandra in her arms just hours after their births. When she'd nursed them each for the first time. It was an emotion she'd nearly forgotten—a rich mingling of joy and pride, relief and expectancy.

"Hello, baby," she whispered. She stroked the dainty fuzz on top of her head. The tiny spirals of black hair were dry now and sprang away from her head in a dark wisp of a halo.

She cuddled the tiny body close to hers. "Oh, sweetheart, you are so precious. I love you so." Tears came—more from frustration than sadness. There were simply no words that could fully express the love Anna felt for this little one.

The urge to nurse the baby was instinctive, but she'd been given something to dry up her milk. Still weak and aching from the birth, she put her knees up in the bed and placed the baby upright in her lap. "Let's look at you, sweetheart," she cooed.

She unwrapped the blanket swaddling the little girl and gently pulled off the booties she wore, unconsciously counting fingers and toes, memorizing the cherubic face. "Oh, you are so beautiful!" She leaned forward and placed a tender kiss on the tiny forehead. The baby scrunched up her face in a scowl. Anna laughed softly at the comical grimace, her heart so tender with love for this child that it ached.

The emotional pain that had hung so heavily on Anna's shoulders before the birth now crept over her anew. They faced a decision of such profound magnitude that it threatened to swallow her.

"Oh, Lord," she prayed, "I give this little girl to you. You and You alone know what lies ahead for her. I know, Father, I *know* that I cannot place her in any more loving hands than Your own. But I'm scared, God…so scared. You know how deeply I love her already. I don't know if I can give her up should You ask that of me."

Hot tears coursed down her cheeks. "Oh, dear God… I don't know if I can give her up. I love her. Oh, how I love her already. Please, show us what to do. Please, Lord. You know we want to do the right thing, but we don't know what that is. We just don't know…"

Looking into the baby's eyes, Anna thought of Justin Walker. This baby probably looked much the way little Justin had as a baby—the deep brown curls and bright dark eyes, the chubby rounded cheeks that Justin still hadn't outgrown. What a blessing that little boy had turned out to be. In many ways, his start in life had been as tragic. A young girl who wasn't yet ready to be a mother, a boy who ran from responsibility. And yet, look how God had redeemed that seeming tragedy. There was much joy and blessing in the Walker home *because* of Justin. And much love there for him, as well. Surely the Walkers' example offered hope for this infant who lay nestled in Anna's lap. Surely somewhere was a family whose love could withstand any prejudice, heal any heartache this little girl would face.

Suddenly, a vision of Tanya Walker's face overwhelmed Anna. Sweet Tanya—such a caring devoted mother. And Daniel—so gentle, yet firm when Justin needed firmness.

And in a blinding, miraculous instant, Anna knew beyond all doubt that this baby—her baby—was meant for Tanya and Daniel Walker. Had been meant for them all along.

Her spirit sang with joy as the answer to their prayers was revealed like a heavy veil being lifted. As though God himself spoke to her, she heard the words in her mind. *This child was not a tragic accident. I had a plan for her little life all along. And you, Anna—you were the instrument I chose to give her life. Because you were obedient, because you suffered for what was right, this will be a blessing, even to you.*

She trembled—not in fear, but in awe. God had redeemed her tragedy in a way she couldn't have imagined. She sat upright in the hospital bed, hugging the baby to her chest, and it seemed as though the room glowed with the aura of God's presence.

For long minutes, she praised Him in utter amazement and joy. The baby fell asleep in her arms, and Anna gently laid her in the bassinet. She lay back on the pillows and watched the soothing rhythms as her baby's chest rose and fell, rose and fell, and she listened to the steady, even breaths that filled the crib beside her. Anna felt herself drifting, until a sleep of perfect peace overtook her.

Because of the Rain

Twenty-two

Paul woke at five o'clock the morning after *Anna's daughter* was born. Anna's daughter. It still seemed unfathomable to him that Anna could have had a child apart from him. Seeing the baby immediately after she was born, Paul knew with certainty that the man who'd been arrested for Anna's rape had indeed fathered the child she'd borne. The baby's appearance left little doubt of that fact.

And yet, when he'd put the infant's tiny hand in his as Anna cuddled her on the delivery bed, he'd felt something rise up in his heart for the baby. Perhaps it was pity or compassion for the uncertainty of her future. But it had felt suspiciously like love. Of course, the baby was a part of Anna, and he loved Anna more deeply now than he'd ever thought possible. Perhaps his feelings for the child sprang from his bond with his wife. Though they'd been living in a nightmare for the past nine months, he and Anna had been drawn together in a precious intimacy that only tragedy could have forged.

He felt strangely suspended in time. Never had he lived

for the moment as he had in these past months. Even now, he could not begin to guess how this would all end.

Although Anna had voiced her longing to raise the child as their own on the day the Whitemans had given up the baby, she'd not acted on that announcement in any way. Of course, by then she'd been so caught up in the physical burden of the pregnancy that Paul knew she'd not been able even to think rationally. But still, she'd seemed unconcerned about preparing a room for the baby, or choosing a name, or even buying one outfit of clothing. Perhaps this was what it meant to trust fully in the Lord. To wait on Him. Paul himself had felt no compulsion to decide the baby's fate. He waited on Anna.

Now, he could scarcely wait to be with her, to find out how the ending of this story—their story—would be written.

—⁓—

It was almost seven-thirty when Paul arrived at the hospital, and breakfast carts were just coming up on the elevator. He walked into Anna's room to find her sitting up in bed, gazing out the large window across from her bed.

"Paul. Oh, honey, I have something to tell you."

"I thought you would, Anna. Somehow I knew you would. I'm ready… I mean that, Anna. I think I'm ready for anything you could tell me." He sat on the bed beside her and took her hand in his.

"They brought her into my room last night, and I held her for a long time, and …" Anna's bottom lip began to quiver. "I'm sorry," she said, her voice breaking. "I didn't want to cry when I told you."

"It's okay, Anna. Cry if you need to." He waited for her to compose herself.

"It…it's going to be so hard. Much harder than I ever dreamed…to let her go, but I know I have to. We have to." Her sentence ended on a sob. She put her fist to her mouth, struggling for composure. "But Paul... I think I know where she belongs."

He gave her a questioning look. He was confused. He'd braced himself to have Anna tell him that she wanted to keep the baby.

Her story poured out now...the vision Anna had of Daniel and Tanya, the conviction that the Walkers were God's plan for the baby all along.

He was truly shocked. Even after they'd learned the identify of Anna's rapist, he'd never thought about the possibility of Daniel and Tanya wanting the baby. And yet, hearing Anna recount her revelation, it seemed to make perfect sense. He squeezed her hand. "I think we've received our answer."

She nodded.

Yet he wanted to be certain that she was making this decision with a clear mind, that she wasn't feeling pressured to make a hasty choice.

He took her face in his hands and looked into her eyes. "Anna, I have to say it one more time. I don't ever want you to look back and feel that I hindered you from keeping this baby. If that's what you truly want, I'm still willing. I mean that with all my heart. Do you understand?"

"Oh, honey, I do. And I love you for it." She fell against him and her tears started anew. "Paul, I could never have gotten through this ordeal without you. You've been everything I could ever ask for through it all. But I know... I know in my heart that this is right. I will never look back. It won't be easy, I know—but I'll never look back. I know this is right."

He enveloped her in his arms, aching for her, for the wrenching decision she had made. Yet so grateful for this answer Anna had received. *They* had received.

They agreed then that Anna would talk to Emma, and together they would offer the child to the Walkers. If Daniel and Tanya accepted, which Paul felt certain they would, he would contact Walter LeMans to begin the legal process for an open adoption.

There was a rap on the door and a young nurse opened it a crack and stuck her head into the room. "Sorry to bother you, but your little one is making a noisy racket down there." She motioned down the hallway toward the nursery. "Would you mind if I hold your breakfast tray while you feed her?"

Paul looked at Anna. "Are you sure it's a good idea to… to get attached?" he asked quietly.

Anna smiled sadly. "It's too late, honey. I'm already attached." To the nurse she said, "Yes, please bring her in."

Paul helped Anna get comfortable, raising the head of the bed and plumping pillows behind her back. Within minutes the nurse reappeared, this time with a squalling infant in her arms.

"Oh, my," Anna laughed softly, her voice quivering. "I forgot how many decibels a hungry baby can generate."

Paul watched as Anna worked with the baby, positioning her across her body until they both seemed comfortable, then gently plying her lips with the warm bottle. Soon the baby was sucking contentedly, and Anna seemed relaxed and contented herself.

As he had when his own daughters were newborns, Paul marveled at the maternal instinct, at how natural and at ease Anna was with the baby.

A great sadness overwhelmed him for what Anna had been asked to endure—and now to give up. For this precious part of her that was his loss as well.

In silence, they sat together until the baby was finished eating. Paul knew, watching her, that Anna was saying goodbye, savoring each moment, committing each tiny feature to memory. And in that instant he felt the need to say his own goodbye. The baby had fallen asleep in Anna's arms, and Paul reached for her.

Anna looked at him with surprise. But with great tenderness, she transferred the infant to his arm. Her tears fell anew as she watched him hold her daughter.

A few minutes later the nurse stuck her head into Anna's room again. "Ah…you got her to sleep," she said, seeing the baby in Paul's arms. She turned to Anna. "Do you feel up to company? You have someone in the waiting room."

Anna looked at Paul as though he might know who was waiting. But he shrugged and shook his head as if to say he hadn't expected anyone.

The nurse disappeared and a few minutes later, Kassandra walked through the doorway. Behind her, looking teary-eyed and uncertain, stood Kara.

Anna gasped in surprise, and then broke into joyous laughter. She had not seen her older daughter in almost eight months. Now, seeing her standing here, looking almost contrite, Anna forgot all that had come between them. She only wanted to take Kara in her arms and hold her.

She reached out, and Kara hurried to her bedside. Anna patted the spot beside her, and Kara met her embrace. They sobbed in each other's arms, neither speaking, but Anna could almost feel the healing taking place.

Across the room, Kassi was absorbed in quiet conversation with Paul, and Anna heard her murmurs of amazement over the baby. When Kassi finally glanced up, Anna smiled at her over Kara's shoulder.

Kara pulled away from Anna and wiped smudges of mascara from her cheeks. "Oh, Mom," she cried, "I'm so glad you're okay."

Anna pulled her close again. She patted Kara's back the way she had when she was a little girl with a scraped knee. How rare these tender moments with her older daughter were. Would they always struggle so to express their love for each other? To allow each other her differences?

Anna drew back and studied Kara. "Do you want to hold the baby?"

Kara stiffened and shook her head. Anna was immediately sorry she'd asked. It would never be easy, but she would have to learn to take what Kara offered and not try to push for more. She was disappointed, and yet, just having Kara here was such an answer to prayer. For now, she would be content with that.

Kassi hurried to Anna's bedside and hugged her. "She's beautiful, Mom, like a little angel." There was awe in her voice.

Paul stood between the girls and pulled them close, one in each arm. "We've decided the baby will go to Daniel and Tanya."

Kassi reached over the bedrail and took the baby's tiny hand in hers. Her shoulders shook and her hair fell over her face in a pale blond curtain that hid the tears Anna knew were falling.

Kara said nothing. They all sat in silence, emotional and unable to speak if they'd wanted to.

After a minute, the baby stirred and opened her eyes. Her tiny fists flailed in the air, and her dark eyes gazed intently at Anna's face.

Anna looked through a veil of tears and saw her family gathered around this child whose advent had nearly torn them apart. They were all weeping openly now, but they were tears that knit them together in an incorruptible bond.

And she realized with surprise that her tears were mostly for joy—for a brand-new daughter safely arrived, for the answer to their prayers—an answer that would give this little one a happy home. For the budding hope of a prodigal daughter's return. And for the love of her precious husband that would carry her through.

There would be a time for sadness, for mournful goodbyes, for a tenuous peace with Kara. But for now, Anna embraced the tenuous joy and let it wash over her like a river.

Twenty-three

Anna knew by the familiar *rat-tat-a-tat-tat* on the door of her hospital room that it was Emma.

"Hello?" Emma's dark head peeked around the door before Anna could answer her knock.

"Emma! I'm so glad you came."

Elegantly dressed in a raw silk suit, its peacock blue sheen beautiful against her ebony skin, Emma wore a wide smile. But Anna detected concern in her eyes as well.

"Anna," she said simply, reaching across the bed to envelope Anna in a hug. She stepped back and studied Anna. "You look wonderful. Now how are you feeling?"

"It was hard, Emma. I'd forgotten what hard work it is to have a baby, or maybe it's just harder at my advanced age." She smiled wanly.

"Well, I'm proud of you. You did a wonderful thing, Anna. I know it was probably the most difficult thing you've ever done, but it was a wonderful thing. Paul tells me the baby is fine."

Anna nodded, her throat too full to speak. She swallowed hard. "Emma...there's something I want to ask you."

Emma looked at her with undisguised curiosity.

"Last night, when they brought the baby in to me, when I...when I held her for the first time, I couldn't get Tanya out of my mind. Emma, I believe this baby might be for Tanya and Daniel. I feel strongly that the Lord might have meant this child for them all along."

Emma's dark eyes widened as she comprehended what Anna was saying.

It was difficult to explain to Emma how strong the impression had been the night before. It was more than just a feeling. She truly believed it had been a divine revelation.

"I don't know if Daniel and Tanya have even thought of having another child," She told Emma, "but Paul and I want to offer this baby to them first. Of course, I don't want them to feel an obligation, but... do you think they might want her?"

"Oh, Anna. Oh, my...there's so much to consider...so much to think about, but...oh, my!" she said again, a broad grin blooming on her face. "I might be wrong, but I don't think they'll be able to get here fast enough! Oh, my! I can hardly believe this!" She embraced Anna again. "I never in my life imagined it would end this way, Anna. Why, I'll be your baby's grandmother!" She clapped her hand over her mouth. "Just listen to me! I'm talking like it's a done deal!"

Emma's joy was infectious, and Anna found herself laughing at her incredulous murmurs. Emma's response confirmed what she'd felt so strongly last night. Still, Daniel and Tanya would have to make the final decision.

—∞—

Emma was with the Walkers when they came to the hospital that night to visit Anna. She'd promised Anna that she wouldn't say anything to them, but Anna could see she was having a difficult time containing her excitement.

Anna had asked Paul to present the idea to Daniel and Tanya. She didn't trust her own emotions. Or her voice. And yet, despite her sadness, there was a strange, deep joy in having such an amazing gift to offer.

Tanya greeted Anna with a warm smile, and Anna thought again how much the young woman looked like her mother. The Walkers had brought flowers for Anna. Pink.

Emma, obviously nervous and about to burst with her secret, busied herself rearranging the bouquet in a clear glass vase. She placed them on the wide windowsill then came to Anna's bedside.

Paul gathered chairs for everyone and when they were seated, he cleared his throat and turned to the young couple.

"There is a special reason why Emma wanted you two to come with her tonight." He winked at Emma, and Anna saw the flicker of a question cross both faces.

"You know that we were hit pretty hard by the news we got two weeks ago. We had peace about the Whitemans adopting this baby. Now, as you know, they've chosen not to take her, knowing she would face discrimination within her own family if they were to adopt her. I don't know if it has ever crossed your minds, or if it's even a possibility for you, but ..." Paul cleared his throat.

Anna watched Tanya's face and saw by her expression of hope mixed with fear, that she'd already guessed what was coming. Tanya reached for Daniel's hand as Paul continued.

"Daniel, Tanya, if you are willing—we don't want to rush you to a decision—but if you are willing, we would like for you to have Anna's baby. Adopt her."

Tanya gasped and put her face in her hands. "Yes! Oh yes," she cried. "We want her. Of course we want her. Oh, Danny, can you believe it?"

Daniel nodded in obvious disbelief. He caressed his wife's shoulders as she leaned across her chair, clinging to him. "I think you have your answer," he said in his quiet, serious way.

"Over these last months," Paul said, "we've seen that your home is full of love. We've seen the fruits of your parenting in little Justin. We both"—he reached for Anna's hand—"we both feel strongly that you are the parents God intended this baby to have."

Daniel swallowed hard and shook his head in obvious disbelief. "I'm humbled," he said simply.

Tanya wept and laughed at the same time.

—⁂—

Anna Grace Walker scrunched up her pudgy face and opened her mouth wide in a huge yawn. She stretched her arms above her head and yawned again. Her bright little eyes darted back and forth between Tanya and Anna, who were bent over either side of the hospital crib, each trying to poke a squirming leg into the tiny pink ruffled sleeper. Tanya cooed to the baby, who blessed her with a silly lopsided grin.

The two women looked at each other as if to say "did you see that smile?" and then they laughed together—the way sisters laughed together.

With deft fingers, Tanya finished fastening the snaps on the little outfit and gently tucked the soft receiving blanket around the baby. "Anna. She's beautiful," Tanya said, a tremor in her voice.

Anna stared down at the baby, afraid to trust her own voice. Finally she said quietly, "She is beautiful, isn't she?" Anna looked up at Tanya. "She'll be so happy with you, Tanya. I know she will."

With outstretched arms, Tanya hurried around to Anna's side of the crib and wrapped her in a hug.

Anna broke down then, her body heaving against the younger woman's embrace. "I'm sorry, Tanya. I know we're doing the right thing. It's…it's just so much harder than I thought it would be."

Wordlessly, Tanya patted her back.

This morning Paul and Anna had signed the papers that would give little Anna Grace over to Daniel and Tanya Walker. There was nothing left for Anna now but to say her goodbyes and go home with Paul.

Already she was longing for Chicago, for the joy of being home again and being truly reunited with her husband.

Daniel and Paul had gone downstairs together—Daniel to bring their car around, Paul to sign Anna out of the hospital. Now both men appeared in the doorway together. There was an uncomfortable moment when no one seemed sure what to do next.

Then, summoning her courage, Anna went to the crib and picked up the baby. Little Anna Grace stirred in her sleep but did not awaken. Anna carried the precious bundle to where Tanya was standing, and with a final caress of the dark curls, she placed the baby tenderly in Tanya's arms.

Now it was Tanya's turn for tears. She wept openly, her tears falling on the baby's blanket. The young mother's tears touched Anna deeply. More eloquently than any words could have, they spoke of Tanya's gratitude for the pain Anna had borne—physical and emotional—so that this child could come into the world, could bring the joy they all knew she would bring to this young family.

Daniel and Tanya had named the baby Anna Grace. "'Grace' because we didn't deserve her, yet God saw fit to give her to us anyway. 'Anna' because we hope she will grow up to be as special as her mother is," Tanya had told Anna that morning.

Anna had grown to love this little family over the difficult months now behind her. The Walkers had given her a priceless gift in naming the baby after her. She would miss them deeply—Tanya especially. Why did life seem to be an endless succession of goodbyes? Anna embraced Tanya again, and the two women wept in each other's arms, the baby cradled between them.

In unison, as if they'd rehearsed, each husband stepped

forward and put a comforting arm around his wife. The unintended choreography of their movements brought a burst of spontaneous laughter, and the solemnity of the moment was lightened.

With an arm still protectively around Anna, Paul said, "Well, I know there's one excited big brother and one very impatient grandma downstairs. We'd better not keep them waiting any longer."

Anna smiled gratefully at her husband and reluctantly maneuvered into the wheelchair that a nurse had brought in. "Regulations, my dear," Paul teased her, and with a flourish, he fell in step beside the nurse who pushed her down the hall toward the elevators.

The elevator doors opened and Daniel and Tanya, baby in arms, stepped into the elevator behind them. Despite the heaviness that remained in Anna's heart, the mood had changed to one of celebration, and she was grateful she could keep her emotions in check. She did not want to dampen the joy of this special family as they welcomed a new little member into their arms. There would be plenty of time later for her to mourn her loss, to truly let the baby go. And, too, there was this unfathomable peace that pervaded her sorrow.

This is right. Never had she felt so sheltered in the center of God's will.

The elevator crept down three floors and opened onto the lobby waiting room. Justin Walker bolted out of his grandmother's custody and tackled his mother with the full force of his twenty-six pounds.

"Whoa! Whoa there, buddy," Daniel cautioned, reaching out a strong arm to steady his wife.

"Is that my new baby?" the little boy asked, looking wide-eyed at the bundle in Tanya's arms.

Daniel looked Anna's way, concern on his face. But she forced a smile and nodded her approval.

Daniel took the sleeping infant from Tanya's arms and knelt down beside his son. "It sure is." His deep voice grew reverent as he made the introduction. "Justin Michael, this is your new baby sister, Anna Grace Walker."

"Hey!" Justin shouted gleefully. "Her name's Anna, just like *our* Anna." He pointed at the wheelchair with a big grin, and Anna's heart stirred at his use of the possessive.

"That's right, Justin," Daniel explained in a low voice. "Remember how we told you Anna helped us get our baby? We wanted the baby to have Anna's pretty name too."

Justin nodded solemnly. "Thanks, Anna," he said politely. Then he skipped over to his mother and hid behind her knees, suddenly bashful.

Emma had come over to where Anna was sitting and let her hand rest on Anna's shoulder. Then she turned to her son-in-law, a sparkle in her eye. "Well, are you going to let me hold that baby, or am I going to have to tear her out of your arms?"

Daniel laughed and handed the baby over to Emma, who clucked and cooed, seeming oblivious to everyone else.

Anna felt a little detached from the whole scene. Here was a family full of joy, sweetly welcoming this tiny newcomer into their lives. Little Anna looked so much a part of them already with her brown skin and her tiny ringlets of dark hair. But it was more than that. It wasn't the physical similarities that made them a family. It was the love that flowed, almost visibly, between them. It was the precious way they'd taken on the guardianship of this child who'd been conceived in violence, born in pain, but now adopted in consummate love. It was the sense that this family had been ordained of God. And again, Anna was overwhelmed with the certainty that this was right—*so very right.*

She felt Paul's strong hands on her shoulders, and she reached up and covered them with her own. Then, blinking back tears of joy and gratitude—and yes, tears of great sorrow, too—she looked up into her husband's eyes and whispered, "Let's go home."

Because of the Rain

Epilogue

Anna came in from the backyard and washed the garden dirt from her hands at the kitchen sink. It was a chilly March afternoon, far too early to be putting out flowers, but the recent rains and a week of unseasonably warm weather had softened the earth and made her anxious to begin the rituals of spring. She had contented herself with pulling weeds and clearing away the pungent mulch of leaves and grass that had covered her garden spot all winter. She rinsed the soap from her hands and looked out the kitchen window. She felt a deep sense of accomplishment—and a little impatience—at the sight of the large rectangle of rich black dirt, now prepared to receive and nourish the seedlings she would plant there a few weeks from now.

The warm weather of the week before had coaxed tightly wrapped buds out of hiding on the branches of the fruit trees that lined the garden's edge. The trees appeared ready to burst into leaf, and Anna feared that the return of March's typical frosty mornings would ruin spring's blossoms. But despite her concern, she couldn't help but revel in the signs that spring's advent was near. Spring was always such a hopeful time.

As she reached for a towel to dry her hands, she heard the sound of Paul's car on the drive and a little thrill went through her. She was always a bit surprised and so grateful that her husband could still have this effect on her after so many years.

She waited at the door to greet him. He came in, briefcase in hand, a light jacket under his arm. He smiled when he saw her waiting there. He put his things down where he stood, reached for her, and drew her into his arms.

"Hi, honey. How was your day?"

"What?" she asked with mock offense. "Didn't you see my garden?"

"I saw it," he said in the teasing voice she loved so well. "Getting a little impatient, aren't we?" He touched a finger playfully to her nose.

"Oh, I am. I can hardly wait to get my flowers out, but at least everything will be ready so I can plant them the minute the weather cooperates."

"Did you get the mail yet?" he asked, changing the subject.

She smiled and pulled away from her husband. "I was far too busy to even think about the mail," she teased. "But sit down, and I'll bring it to you."

How wonderful it was to talk of the weather and the day's mail—the mundane things of life that she now relished.

She walked through the living room out to the front porch and pulled a bundle of mail from the box beside the door. Absently, she sorted through the usual stack of catalogs and junk mail, culling the important bills and letters from the pile as she walked back into the house.

As she laid a small stack of catalogs and magazines aside on the table in the dining room, a small ivory envelope fell to the floor. She picked it up and glanced curiously at the return address. *Walker...New Haven, Indiana...* It was from Tanya!

"Paul, come here!" Her hands were shaking as she tore open the envelope.

She unfolded the letter and pulled a photograph from the thin sheaf of pages. Paul came up beside her and peered over her shoulder. Two bright pairs of eyes smiled at them from the glossy snapshot. There was Justin, his black springs of hair defying a new close-cropped haircut, a broad smile on his pudgy face. His arms were wrapped possessively around a beautiful little girl. She wore a frilly red dress that framed her dark face with lace and ribbons. She had chubby arms and legs, and one of her booties had fallen off revealing tiny, fat, perfect toes. Her hair was lighter than Justin's—heathery shades of brown—but it grew in tight spiraled ringlets like her brother's. Her wide smile matched his, except hers was toothless and full of bubbles.

This is my baby girl!

Anna leaned heavily against the table, her heart beating rapidly. She felt light-headed. She leaned back against her husband and gazed at the picture. Trembling, she smoothed the creases in Tanya's letter and held it up for Paul to read with her.

She felt his arms tighten around her, and through a wavering curtain of tears, she began to read. She could almost hear Tanya's deep resonant voice speak the words that filled the page in the young mother's elegant handwriting.

March 19

Dear Anna,

You can see how quickly Anna Grace is growing. She weighs almost fourteen pounds now, and in spite of being so chubby, she's quite the little acrobat! She rocks back and forth on her tummy until she gets wedged in the corner of her crib, then she cries for us to rescue her. I had a little step stool by the bed so Justin could watch her, but when we found him hanging over the crib rail trying to pick her up one morning, we had to hide the stool away! Two little ones are keeping me on my toes more than I ever imagined, but I'm loving every minute of it.

We still can scarcely believe the unexpected blessing little Anna has been in our lives, Daniel and I stand by her crib before we go to bed each night and marvel at the way she came to be here. Oh, Anna, I hope you and Paul know how right you were to give this little girl life! She is a marvelous answer to our prayers—prayers we'd barely begun to voice yet—and we thank the Lord every minute for bringing her—and you—into our lives!

Justin loves Anna fiercely and will hardly let anyone else near her. And she lights up whenever he comes into a room— kicks her feet and grins from ear to ear. Already she seems to know that he is someone special. I am so grateful that he will grow up having a little sister to love and that she will grow up having the big brother I never had. I guess every little girl longs for an older brother (unless she has one, Mom would say! Ha ha!)

Anna smiled, remembering Emma's stories of three older brothers who tormented her mercilessly. Emma had become such a dear friend. Anna marveled at the way the barriers had come down between them. It seemed strange that they'd once felt uncomfortable with their differences. Through the pain of the past months, Emma had been an anchor for Anna, and now, she was a precious tie to the child Anna had borne. It comforted her to think of Emma rocking the baby, giving her the loving attention only a grandmother could.

Anna finished Tanya's letter, then sat down at the table to read it through again. In her matter-of-fact way, Tanya had given Anna all the little details that a mother longed to know. The baby was happy and healthy. Little Anna was loved beyond anything she and Paul could have hoped for. The circumstances of her birth were no longer of any consequence. Only the joy she had brought this little family mattered now. Only the *blessing* remained.

Silently Anna handed the letter to Paul, and with the

photograph in hand, she stood and went into the kitchen. He followed her and watched as she tucked the photo in a corner of the bulletin board on the wall beside the phone. She could hardly wait to show it to the girls. Kara and Kassi would both be home for a weekend visit soon.

Anna glanced at the calendar that hung in the center of the corkboard. Its precise squares were filled once again with meetings and appointments, social events, and her busy class schedule. She even had a lunch date with Maggie Ryan. She held firmly to the hope that the rift in her friendship with Maggie could yet be mended.

Yes, the calendar was full, and their lives had resumed a comforting sense of normalcy. They were healing—slowly they were healing—and life was becoming rich and fulfilling again.

Her eyes fell on today's date: *March 21.*

"Oh, Paul," Anna breathed, pointing to the date.

Exactly one year ago today, she had lain wounded and violated in a dark Orlando alley. If they'd known on that day the cross they would be asked to carry, Anna wasn't sure they could have gone on. But now, in God's perfect timing, Tanya's letter had arrived, confirming His goodness, His grace, and most of all, His redeeming power. God had turned the tribulation of the past year into something beautiful. He had given them beauty for ashes, the oil of joy for mourning. He had been glorified. And they would never be the same.

Paul pulled her again into his embrace, and Anna heard the emotion in his voice. "We did the right thing, didn't we, Anna?" It was almost a whisper.

She fell into her husband's arms and wept for joy.

DEBORAH RANEY dreamed of writing a book since the summer she read Laura Ingalls Wilder's Little House books and discovered that a Kansas farm girl could, indeed, grow up to be a writer. After a happy twenty-year detour as a stay-at-home mom, Deb penned her first novel, *A Vow to Cherish*, which won a Silver Angel Award and inspired the acclaimed World Wide Pictures film of the same title. Since then, her books have won the RITA Award, HOLT Medallion, ACFW Carol Award, National Readers' Choice Award, as well as twice being finalists for the Christy Award. Deb teaches at writers' conferences across the country. She and her husband, Ken Raney, recently traded small-town life in Kansas —the setting of many of Deb's novels—for life in the (relatively) big city of Wichita. They have four children and a growing brood of precious grandchildren who all live much too far away. Visit Deb on the Web at www.deborahraney.com.

Other Books by Deborah Raney

STAND-ALONE NOVELS
A Scarlet Cord
A Nest of Sparrows
Over the Waters
Insight
Above All Things
The Face of the Earth
Silver Bells
Because of the Rain (first published as In the Still of Night)
Nearly (first published as Kindred Bond)

SERIES
A Vow to Cherish • Within This Circle

The Camfield Novels
Beneath a Southern Sky • After The Rains
Breath of Heaven (coming soon)

The Clayburn Novels
Remember to Forget • Leaving November • Yesterday's Embers

The Hanover Falls Novels
Almost Forever • Forever After • After All

The Chicory Inn Novels
Home to Chicory Lane • Two Roads Home • Another Way Home
Close to Home • Home at Last

NOVELLAS
"Circle of Blessings" in A Prairie Christmas Collection
"A January Bride" in Winter Brides
"Going Once..." in A Kiss is Still a Kiss
"Finally Home" in Missouri Memories

To learn more, visit:
deborahraney.com

Made in the USA
Lexington, KY
15 June 2019